HERO.COM

ANDY BRIGGS
HERO.COM

Virus
Attack

Walker & Company New York

First published in Great Britain in 2008 by Oxford University Press
Published in the United States of America in January 2010 by
Walker Publishing Company, Inc., a division of Bloomsbury Publishing, Inc.
Visit Walker & Company's Web site at www.bloomsburykids.com

For information about permission to reproduce selections from this book, write to
Permissions, Walker & Company, 175 Fifth Avenue, New York, New York 10010

Library of Congress Cataloging-in-Publication Data
Briggs, Andy.
Virus attack / Andy Briggs.
p.   cm. — (Hero.com)
Summary: Arch fiends Basilisk and the Worm try to destroy the Hero Foundation by first bringing
down the Web site from which teenagers Toby, Pete, Lorna, and Emily download their superpowers.
ISBN-13: 978-0-8027-9484-0 • ISBN-10: 0-8027-9484-X
[1. Superheroes—Fiction. 2. Computer viruses—Fiction.
3. Adventure and adventurers—Fiction.] I. Title.
PZ7.B76528Vi 2010   [Fic]—dc22   2009007462

Printed in the U.S.A. by Quebecor World Fairfield, Pennsylvania
2 4 6 8 10 9 7 5 3 1

For Sab—
a real hero!

From: Andy Briggs
To: HERO.COM readers everywhere
Subject: Careful on the Web!

As you know, the Internet is a brilliant invention, but you need to be careful when using it.

In this awesome book, the heroes (and villains!) download their powers from different Web sites. But HERO.COM and VILLAIN.NET don't really exist. :-(
I thought them up when I was dreaming about how cool mind control would be. The idea for HERO.COM suddenly came to me—especially the scene where Lorna and Emily . . . Oh wait! You haven't read it yet so I'd better shut up! :-) Anyway, I began writing and before I knew it, the idea had spiraled into VILLAIN.NET as well. But I had to make up all of the Internet stuff. None of it is really out there on the Web.

Here are my tips for safe surfing on the Web: keep your identity secret (like all good superheroes do); stick to safe Web sites; make sure a parent, teacher, or guardian knows that you're online—and if anyone sends you anything that makes you feel uncomfortable, don't reply, and tell an adult you trust.

I do have my own Web site, and it's totally safe (even without superpowers!):
www.heroorvillainbooks.com

Be safe out there!

:-)

CONTENTS

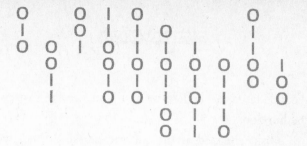

A Second Chance

The sky was dark as gray plumes of ash and steam rose from the ocean, and yet a glimmer of sunlight poked through the haze. It offered just enough light for the burned figure to see his next handhold as he pulled himself farther up the hill that jutted above the blazing jungle.

What seemed like hours earlier, but could well have been only minutes, Basilisk had been running for his life from a superhero. He'd managed to lose his pursuer in the dense jungle, aided by the volcano smoke that blanketed the landscape. But it had cost him several injuries, and he'd almost broken his leg when he'd fallen down a ravine.

At the top of the hill he fought for his breath and watched a twin-rotor Chinook helicopter land on the beach. Even through the volcanic atmosphere the Enforcers' logo was visible on the side. The shape-shifting reptilian superhero called Chameleon was easily recognizable as he climbed onto the tail ramp. Fifteen seconds later the helicopter rose and vanished toward the horizon.

Basilisk wheezed as the sulfuric smoke drifted over him. He had never thought his life would end on a plateau above a sea of flowing lava. He reflected on his childhood, long ago in Hungary, when he had sneaked from the small hut that he called home to watch shooting stars light up the night sky. His mind's eye replayed the moment one of the stars grew bigger, illuminating the landscape until it drove into the earth in a blinding explosion.

He didn't know it, but the light was high-intensity radiation, although at the time the concept of radiation wasn't yet understood. The radiation burned his eyes and mutated his body in ways that he'd only just come to understand centuries later. He thought that he'd been blinded. His father had found him and thrown water across the boy's face to wake him. Then he pried his eyes open—unleashing his child's new powers. In a bright burst of blue light his father turned to stone under the boy's gaze.

Basilisk shook his head sadly. That was the moment his life switched from normality, and he embraced the villain within him.

That was the day Basilisk was born.

Ironically, the man who could turn others to stone was about to be killed on an island that was fast becoming liquid rock. The fumes must have been getting to him, since the ground felt as if it was sliding away. For a second Basilisk thought the plateau was crumbling—but it *was* moving. Tiny stones were dancing from every direction toward a central point where the earth began to bulge. Then a figure rose from the ground, constructed of millions of flowing dirt particles.

Basilisk watched the hallucination in silence as it formed a squat figure, a little over three feet tall and wearing loose, flowing crimson robes. A dazzling brooch, forming a spiraling worm design, hypnotically reflected the weak rays of the sun. As the last clumps of dirt constructed the newcomer, an almost inhuman face was revealed: a blunt head with a wide flat nose, two holes instead of ears, and not a single strand of hair.

Basilisk fixated on the brooch, which seemed to spin, drawing him in, clouding his mind. He snapped his gaze away, breaking the brooch's hypnotic power. Recognition flickered across Basilisk's face.

"Am I dead?" he said in a hoarse voice. "I must be. I know you died long ago, Worm!"

Worm looked at Basilisk with a humorless smile. When he spoke it seemed the words came out as a sigh.

"You're not dead or going crazy. Luckily for you, I wasn't killed. I was trapped; entombed during the war. I was held in a frozen state of cryogenic sleep, only recently enjoying a new breath of freedom. I must say, I am shocked to see how the world has changed so drastically. But I have found my talents still useful, even in this modern world."

Basilisk shook his head. He knew Worm's history—or at least the history of supervillains. "'Worm is the most despicable rogue to have foiled the Allies during the Second World War,'" he quoted. "At least you were, until Commander Courage killed you."

"Commander Courage? Ha! What a heartless soul that hero was! He didn't kill me, obviously! He left me there, *forgotten*." Anger flashed on the villain's face. "You shouldn't believe *everything* you read in the history books, especially as I plan to rewrite them. But that is another matter. I see since I was here last that the Council of Evil has taken control of world crime."

Basilisk tried to laugh, but it came out as a dry cough. Hours earlier he had been unfolding his plan to bring the Council of Evil down, but it had all gone terribly wrong. "The Council is a bunch of ignorant fools."

"I agree! What a stupid idea the Council is! Almost seventy years I was in frozen sleep, and the first thing they ask for when I awake is a permit! A *permit*? To conduct evil? I was flabbergasted! It's all red tape and form filling now. Whatever happened to holding countries to ransom at breakfast and trying to destroy the moon by dinner? I should get myself on the Council so I have influence over them. Show them that the *old ways* were the best." Worm circled as he talked, and Basilisk couldn't help but notice the soil and rock stuck to his feet like molasses.

"And what better way to get them to trust me than by turning you in? They're offering a plump reward for you. Dead or alive."

Basilisk grunted, but he stopped as a sharp pain shot through his ribs from the effort. "You're nothing more than a glorified bounty hunter now? How the mighty have fallen."

Worm stopped circling and jabbed a finger at Basilisk. "Remember I said dead *or* alive. I have no preference either way."

Basilisk's body was aching, but his mind was still sharp. He knew Worm was once a respected criminal mastermind, but he was definitely out of his element in the modern world. However, he was Basilisk's only ticket off this island; all he had to do was convince Worm not to deliver him to the Council. Besides, Worm had powers that Basilisk suspected might be of use for his own schemes.

Basilisk held up his hands in a feeble gesture. "Wait! We both agree that the Council of Evil needs to change. But it's too strong to attack directly. Believe me, I've tried. There is an alternative, however."

Worm's curiosity was piqued. "Continue."

"The Council is creating new villains through Villain.net."

Worm nodded. His brief introduction to the Internet had left him thoroughly bewildered, but he didn't want Basilisk to know that. "I am aware of this. I was told there were fewer Primes being born with superpowers than there used to be. It's a sensible solution to ensure our survival."

"But the Hero Foundation has their own Web site to recruit heroes. And Commander Courage runs it."

Worm bristled at the mention of the superhero. It was bad enough to discover that the hero who had imprisoned him for almost seventy years was still alive, but that he was leading the Hero Foundation—a group he had established during the Second World War— added insult to injury.

Basilisk saw Worm's fists clench, and an expression of hatred cloud his ugly features. Despite the pain racking his body, Basilisk smiled. He always had been gifted at manipulating people. He recalled the plan his protégé, Jake Hunter, had suggested. Based on a school prank, but possessing a kernel of genius: "Hero.com is the Foundation's main line of defense. If we launch a virus attack on the Hero.com site, it will cripple it long enough for us to be able to launch an assault on the Hero Foundation without being hindered by any unwelcome superheroes."

Worm nodded, although he didn't fully understand

what Basilisk meant. "And I can kill Courage with my own hands."

"With Commander Courage dead, *we* can control the Foundation. Bring Hero.com back online as our own weapon and use it to battle the Council of Evil—head-to-head."

The plan had been percolating in Basilisk's mind since the moment Jake Hunter had suggested it to him. Better still, with Hunter out of the picture, it was an idea he could claim as his own. "Think about it, Worm. A world with no heroes and no way to make anymore. We'd be as powerful as the Council."

Worm made a *harrumph* noise from the back of his throat as he considered the suggestion. "I must admit to being a little *behind* modern jargon after having been locked away for so long. I won't pretend to know precisely what you mean."

Basilisk sighed. He didn't have the energy to explain the advent of computer technology and the origin of the Internet from its humble beginnings as a secret U.S. government project. But Worm's ignorance could be used to Basilisk's advantage. "That's why you need me. I lived through this technological boom. There is little I don't know."

Worm considered the idea a bit more. It boiled down to revenge on his most hated enemy, coupled with the fact that if he ran the Foundation, then he could operate without the meddlesome Council of Evil breathing down his neck.

"I could use a sidekick," Worm mused. Basilisk flinched at the very mention of being a sidekick, but luckily Worm didn't notice. Across the island, cloaked by billowing clouds of ash, the volcano loudly erupted once more. The ground shook furiously.

Worm finally made up his mind.

"And you think this *technological* scheme will work?"

Basilisk used the last of his strength to prop himself up on his elbow. "I assure you. I have a three-phase plan to bring down *every* hero on this planet and crush the Hero Foundation once and for all. Then once *we* resurrect Hero.com under our own control, the Council will be unable to stop us. The world would be ours for the taking! Then you could conduct your own brilliant plans *unhindered*." Basilisk hated being sycophantic, but it did serve his purpose right now.

Worm nodded with the slight hint of a smile. "So be it. Let us leave this infernal place."

Without warning he grabbed Basilisk's arm. Basilisk felt a tickling sensation as his atoms began to vibrate and disperse. Both figures rapidly dissolved into fine particles that vanished into the quaking ground.

All in a Day's Work

The rusted bow of a battered cargo vessel churned through the ocean, its destination a sliver of land on the horizon. Faded lettering on the dented bow revealed the ship's name: The *Watchman*. It moved with no running lights on, making it a black whale cutting through the sea. Dense smoke poured from its weatherworn funnel, but otherwise the vessel looked abandoned. At first glance, no one would have suspected that the crew were all ruthless smugglers, armed with automatic weapons and not a conscience among them.

They were being tracked by three superheroes silently flying above. The heroes were all thinking the same thing—the automatic weapons below were nowhere near as dangerous as the fact that they were out way past their parents' curfews. The consequences of that were too dire to contemplate.

Toby squinted, trying to make out more detail on the boat. He regretted not having tried to download some kind of night-vision power from Hero.com. But then again, he'd had no idea they would be out so late—plus he wasn't sure what the stick-figure icon for it would be. He just hoped none of them had downloaded any useless powers, as they sometimes did.

Lorna and Emily flew close on either side, talking in low voices.

"I'm getting cold," complained Lorna. Having learned from previous adventures, they were all dressed in thick black clothes, but the chill still permeated.

Toby didn't bother replying. Over the last few weeks his sister's complaints had increased with each job they had downloaded from Hero.com. His best friend, Pete, had even started to agree with her, which wasn't good news. Luckily Pete wasn't within earshot. Toby glanced around, suddenly aware that his friend had been gone longer than he'd anticipated. He glanced at the lights on the horizon.

"We're running out of time," he warned. "We can't wait for Pete. We have to stop this thing now."

"It's a massive boat. How are we supposed to stop it?" said Emily.

"Why bother? This is something we should leave for the police," Lorna grumbled.

"Police don't patrol out here," Toby snapped back.

"The coast guard, or customs, or border patrol or whatever you call it. What's the point in having these great powers if we're just stopping *normal* people?

All in a Day's Work

What about the supervillains out there? We're supposed to be fighting *them*."

Toby rolled his eyes. "It was on the job board and it needed to be done."

The list of jobs on Hero.com seemed to be growing by the day, although not every job was a direct result of an errant supervillain. "Besides, I thought we decided after the trouble with Doc Tempest that we should take things a little easier?"

"*You* decided, Toby," Lorna retorted.

Emily tried to avoid getting involved with the argument. Which was just as well, as she detected movement on the deck below. Figures had left a cabin and were running to the bow of the ship. The moonlight glinted tellingly off the rifles they carried in both hands.

"Shush, you two! Look, they're coming out!" she said—maybe a little too loudly. One of the figures looked up and began yelling in Spanish. He pointed at the three figures with the barrel of his rifle.

Toby realized with dread that, while arguing, they had moved so that the moon was *behind* them—highlighting their silhouettes so the men below could easily spot them.

"Down!" he yelled.

They all plummeted just as the dull clatter of gunfire broke out across the deck. Bullets shrieked through the air—too close for comfort.

Toby dived straight for the ocean's surface, aware that he hadn't downloaded any power that would render him bulletproof. He was so low that foam from the boat's wake soaked his chest. He glanced up to see that Lorna had thrown up a protective shield of energy that rippled as bullets harmlessly struck it. Emily cowered close behind her. *Typical of Lorna to pick a defensive power*, thought Toby. Not that selecting powers on Hero.com was a straightforward process.

Chameleon, the only heroic Prime that Toby had ever met, had told them there was an instruction manual on the Web site. When he'd eventually found it, Toby had been baffled by the complex jargon used. He did learn that the stick figure icons, which represented the powers, were laid out with *some* degree of logic. Lorna always seemed smart enough to pick the most useful powers for their missions, whereas he just chose the most fun-looking ones.

His thoughts were interrupted as a deckhand leaned over the gunwale of the ship and spotted him. Toby could make out the square night-vision goggles the man wore. The muzzle flash of the weapon flickered and a stream of bullets zipped past him.

Time to end this, he thought.

Toby barrel-rolled to one side to make himself less of a target. He extended his hands and fine black tendrils shot from his fingertips, each no wider than a strand of cotton, but bunched together they were as thick as rope. The sticky tendrils splattered against the man's night-vision goggles and the gun. Toby yanked the strands back, tearing the equipment from him. He shook his hands and the strands broke away, falling into the sea. The startled man stared in Toby's direction as if he'd just seen a ghost, then spun around and ran across the deck, shouting in panic.

Above, Emily peeked around Lorna's energy shield and flicked her hands. A pair of golden orbs, no bigger than Ping-Pong balls, sprang from her palms and raced toward the crew. She watched in fascination as the heat-seeking orbs were guided toward two men, striking them in the chest. The orbs exploded with a dull *plop* and the men were catapulted across the deck. They slammed into the bulkhead, weapons skittering away.

A third man gaped as his colleagues were blown aside, and then looked up as if realizing for the first time that the two girls were suspended in the air as if by magic. He hesitated in firing—giving Emily an opportunity to fire another set of golden orbs.

The man dropped his weapon and fled. He glanced behind him to see the orbs were weaving across the deck in his direction. He skidded around a corner leading to the main cabins and checked behind him. The orbs were relentlessly pursuing. He increased his pace and threw himself into an open cabin door, pushing his whole body against the steel door to close it.

Both orbs hit the door with such thunderous force that the metal buckled and the door was blasted from its hinges. The warped steel propelled the man across the cabin and into the far wall, knocking him unconscious.

Toby gained altitude to join Emily and Lorna.

"I thought there would be more of them," said Toby. "And I thought pirates would be a lot tougher."

"Wrong type of pirates," said Lorna in her best "ye olde pirate" accent.

"It's turning!" exclaimed Emily. As they watched, the boat increased speed and began to slide in the water. "Must be somebody at the wheel."

Toby felt slightly disappointed at what seemed like an easy victory—he had been expecting the mission to be a lot more fun, but knew better than to say so out loud. "We didn't need Pete after all, the slacker. Let's get onto the boat and stop it."

Toby wondered if Pete was okay. The last time he'd seen him was when Pete had plummeted underwater several minutes ago, convinced he had downloaded aquatic powers. Toby wasn't too concerned, since Pete was a strong swimmer. Besides, his friend had been acting differently since they had been using the superpowers. Toby just hoped being a hero wasn't going to his head, like it was with his sister.

All in a Day's Work

They edged forward toward the ship's dark helm at the front of the boat. As they drew nearer they could see the captain inside the control room, bathed in pale lights. The captain didn't look around, but instead stared at his instruments. The ship was old enough to be steered by a large wheel, instead of the small computer joysticks of modern vessels. The captain was using all his weight to keep the wheel level.

Toby landed on the raised deck and took a step forward when Lorna suddenly gave a loud yelp. She had been about to follow her brother through the control room door when she was violently dragged up and backward into the sky by some invisible force. She suddenly stopped and hung stationary for a second, before rapidly zigzagging through the air like a balloon—coming to another abrupt halt. She stopped screaming for a microsecond before plummeting into the water.

Lorna's screams alerted the captain. He spun around to see Toby—who had his back to the man, watching his sister's plight. He didn't see the captain pick up a small fire extinguisher and raise it to strike Toby's head.

Emily dragged her gaze from Lorna, who was thrashing in the ocean, to Toby, who was about to be clocked by the captain.

"Tobe!" she screamed and extended her hands. The orbs appeared as before—but then they popped like harmless soap bubbles. For a brief second she panicked—the friends' powers were only temporary and liable to run out at any moment. But she reasoned that her powers hadn't expired, or else she wouldn't still be flying.

Toby heard her warning and turned just as the captain swung the fire extinguisher down. Toby ducked aside but the extinguisher still clipped his shoulder. The might of the attack forced him to the floor, his right arm numb from where he'd been struck. The captain loomed over him and hissed in an unfamiliar language. Toby could see the bloodthirsty rage in the man's eyes. . . .

A sound like a million waterfalls rumbling interrupted the captain. After years on the sea, he knew trouble from the ocean when he heard it. He looked through the control room's window. Toby followed the captain's gaze, his eyes widening.

A wall of water rose in front of the ship, almost one hundred feet tall and four times as wide. It was a tidal wave—except this one didn't move, but stood up from the sea like a liquid wall, seawater rising on one side and cascading down the other. The cap of the wave bubbled and frothed, betraying the force of the water contained beneath—and Pete stood on top of it like a champion surfer. Dressed in his black wetsuit with his arms folded, he was laughing in delight.

Once they had accepted the mission to stop a pirate vessel from smuggling its illegal cargo into the country,

All in a Day's Work

Pete had scoured the Web site for aquatic powers. It had delayed them by a good forty minutes as he struggled to make an educated guess about which icons symbolized them.

The moment they had found the freighter, Pete had plummeted into the ocean. He had been delighted to discover he could breathe just as well underwater as in the air. While the others tracked the ship from above, it had taken him time to discover what other powers he had. After some experimentation, Pete succeeded in scaring a school of inquisitive fish when he created a dense ball of seawater that was almost as hard as rock.

When the fight broke out above, he exerted himself to create a wall of water so he could stop the ship. And he was surprised to see that it had worked a lot better than he'd imagined.

Emily was the only one with a clear vantage point above the action. The tidal wave Pete had created was huge, and she was certain that it was well beyond the limits of the powers they were *supposed* to have.

"How can he do that?" she muttered to herself.

She checked that Lorna was still treading water to the right of the ship—*starboard*, she corrected herself. Toby was still on his knees outside the door.

When she looked back at Pete she saw him draw his hands together as though he were closing curtains—and the tidal wave surged forward.

She yelled, "Pete, no, don't do it!"

The weight of the tidal wave would surely crush Toby on the ship and Lorna in the water, and it didn't seem that Pete had any idea either of them was in there.

Pete was enjoying himself too much to notice Emily frantically waving her arms in warning, and the roar of the water was too loud for him to hear her.

Without thinking, Emily dived toward the ocean.

Pete was stunned at the wave's magnitude, but he assumed that he was controlling his powers like a true master. The wave tore forward. As it reached the bow of the freighter he noticed movement from the corner of his eye—it was Emily flying down. Pete looked around with a frown, suddenly aware that none of his friends were airborne.

Toby clambered to his feet, holding a deck rail as the tidal wave struck the boat. The front of the vessel was pitched almost vertically up. Toby's feet slipped from the deck and he fell. The angled floor now became a slide and he plummeted down toward a set of steel railings that circled the control tower. He hit them hard, the impact knocking the breath out of him.

His shoulder was aching so much that he could only use one hand to try and right himself as the wave carried the ship backward through the ocean at an acute angle. The water broke overhead and rained down on

All in a Day's Work

the deck like a heavy downpour that increased in intensity with every passing second.

Salt water stung Toby's eyes and his mouth tasted of nothing else. He pushed himself forward to fly—but found the superpower had vanished. He suddenly felt helpless, as the world around him became nothing but seawater and a frenzy of white bubbles.

Emily had to use both hands to heave Lorna from the water. It was difficult to gain any altitude with the additional weight.

"Higher!" shouted Lorna as the wave enveloped the boat.

"I can't! You're too heavy!"

"What?" Lorna bit back any argument over her weight. Now was not the time to fight. Emily opted to try to outrun the wave instead. Lorna felt the world starting to move in slow motion as the surge bore down on them. They watched in amazement as the water submerged the vessel—and then the entire wall fell back into the ocean as though somebody had pressed a "stop" button. The colossal sound of collapsing water dissipated into silence.

Lorna suddenly jolted into the air, bouncing off Emily, as her own flying power kicked back into action. She hovered next to her friend and they watched the surface of the sea bubble where the ship *used* to be. Personal possessions floated to the surface along with eight struggling crew members who all treaded water that was fast becoming littered with thousands of DVD cases. They spread across the surface like driftwood as they escaped from the smuggler ship's hold.

Pete swooped down next to the girls.

"Wow! Wasn't I incredible? Did you see what I did? Amazing!"

Emily looked incredulous. "That was a *team* effort." But Pete wasn't listening. He'd become boastful of his own exploits on the last few missions they had completed. It was beginning to get annoying.

Pete suddenly looked around with concern. "Where's Toby?"

Emily pointed. "He was *on* the boat, you idiot."

They stared at the surface for a stunned second— then Pete flew straight for the water . . .

And bounced right off, as if he had flown into a sheet of rubber. He rolled across the undulating surface, not a centimeter of his body getting wet.

Lorna and Emily watched with concern. The boat crew were swimming normally, but Pete couldn't break the surface. It was like kneeling on a bouncy castle as he pounded the mysteriously solid water.

"I can't break through!" he yelled.

Emily suddenly understood. "Our powers are malfunctioning!"

A loud splash sent Pete reeling backward as Toby

surfaced through the plastic cases, sucking in a deep breath.

"Dude!" Pete said as he stood on the water—which suddenly collapsed under him, sending him splashing into the ocean as the laws of physics decided to wake up. He treaded water next to Toby.

"You okay?"

Toby nodded. He glanced around and saw the captain had surfaced some ways away and was frantically swimming toward his crew.

"You planning on swimming in there all night?" asked Lorna. She was grinning with relief.

Pete and Toby flew from the water to join the girls. Toby looked around the ocean and got a sense of what had happened. The water was littered with cases and the ship's crew, who were trying to distance themselves from the superheroes. Aside from other debris, there was no sign of the freighter. In the distance, a spotlight combed the water, and they heard the dull drone of an approaching coast guard vessel.

"Sinking the boat still counts as stopping it, right?" Pete asked.

"We stopped them from smuggling the pirated movies," said Emily. "That's a successful mission."

"Still think it's a waste of time though," said Lorna. The others looked at her. "Well it is! You nearly died, Tobe. For what?"

"For doing what superheroes do."

"And we get a bunch of Heroism points," Pete added.

Lorna shook her head. "That's my point. We did what the authorities should be doing. Okay, that may be heroic but it's not the job of a *superhero*. We should be doing bigger things. Getting ourselves *noticed*."

Toby rolled his eyes. This was Lorna's latest argument. She wanted to use the powers to get famous instead of to do a job. "We've talked about this. Getting noticed is the last thing we want. If people knew we had these powers or that superheroes even existed . . ." He drifted off.

"Exactly. What would happen?" said Lorna. "We might get a little fame and even get paid to do this stuff. I'd rather go on a talk show and brag about what we've done than do a paper route."

"I agree," said Pete.

Toby shot Pete a look. Agreeing with his sister was a huge betrayal. "We've been through this before." Toby sighed. "There are government departments and the Enforcers out there trying to stop the public from knowing!"

"And what else are they hiding?" said Pete, eager for a conspiracy theory.

"Anyway, there's more important things to think about," said Emily, who was tiring of the constant fighting. "Like why did our powers glitch?"

All in a Day's Work

Pete shrugged. "I felt terrific. Better than ever. Except when I bounced off the water. *That* was strange."

"They were a little *too* good," Emily commented.

"Jealous?"

"No. I'm just saying. Don't you think your powers seemed, I don't know, *increased*, while ours suffered?"

Pete swapped a glance with Toby and nodded. "She's jealous all right."

Emily looked away, refusing to argue. The coast guard vessel was drawing nearer. Its searchlight drifted across the sea and fixed on one of the crew, who was frantically signaling for help.

"We better get going," said Toby. "Our job here is done."

The superheroes rose into the night sky and headed toward home. If the coast guard crew had had sharper hearing, they might have heard the sound of arguing passing overhead as four figures shot across the full moon.

Moonlight played over the swaying heather fields of the Cornish Lizard Peninsula in Cornwall, England. Powerful floodlights pierced the dark landscape and bathed the world's largest and oldest satellite earth station: England's massive Goonhilly Downs complex. Some sixty-one satellite dishes of all shapes and sizes poked toward the heavens. In the center of the complex stood multiple buildings that housed every-thing from the tourist center to the control rooms. It was a twenty-four-hour operation, so even at this time of night there was a full contingent of staff on duty, but at least the external roads were quiet. A lone security jeep rolled by; the guard inside had little idea that there were intruders already within the complex.

One of the large control rooms designated to obscure the dish array was a hybrid of older decor and modern computers. The night staff lay unconscious on the floor, with one unlucky soul transformed to stone when he had tried to contact security. The telephone was still clenched in his petrified hand.

Basilisk was slumped in a chair, leaning on the central Y-shaped desk as he stared at a computer screen. After a few weeks spent formulating their plan at Worm's base, he was dismayed that he still hadn't fully recovered from his ordeal on the volcanic island. His leg throbbed, forc-ing him to walk with a cane. His new dark-green body-suit hid the scars well and the deep hood of his cloak obscured his badly burned face—a face so damaged that even he no longer recognized it. His regeneration powers should have kicked in by now, but nothing had hap-pened. It was time for a fresh regeneration—a completely new set of DNA to rejuvenate him as it had over the cen-turies. But right now, that would have to wait.

Worm stood across from him, examining a large

monitor displaying the site's numerous satellite arrays. Worm was bowled over by the leap in progress that had occurred during his incarceration and was taking every opportunity to marvel at it.

"Incredible," he muttered under his breath. "Truly amazing. Who would have thought mankind could do all this and finally set foot in space without the aid of superpowers?"

Basilisk shook his head. He had done his best to bring Worm up-to-date on over half a century's achievements, but the technology was far beyond anything Worm had dreamed of. His constant exclamations of astonishment were wearing Basilisk down. Still, Basilisk had lost everything when his island was destroyed and was forced to rely on Worm. The villain's unique skills were now integral to Basilisk's plan.

Worm's powers allowed him to travel through earth, ideally soil or sand, by deconstructing himself into billions of cell particles and seeping through the ground—*in between* the very particles that made the earth seem solid. By altering his technique he could just as easily walk through tiny cracks in the walls or seep under doors to enter rooms, but there was nothing technological about his powers. The drawback was that they weren't very effective through dense material such as rock or metal.

Once they had left the island, Basilisk and Worm had spent weeks gathering equipment, such as laptops and

Basilisk's new body armor, so they could implement the ambitious plan.

Basilisk had worked with Worm to teach him how to adapt his powers to use on computers. It had been a slow process, especially with Worm's constant complaints and his threats to hand Basilisk over to the Council of Evil every time something went wrong. But eventually, under careful guidance from Basilisk, Worm was able to use his ability to send atomized fragments of his finger into a computer. His power was limited; he could only extend so far before the pain became unbearable. Scrambling his body through the dirt was easy, but the metal was denser and electronic systems had magnetic fields and electron flows yanking at his every atom—it was like swimming through a riptide that threatened to pull you apart. But his reach of a dozen inches was enough to enter the heart of a processor chip—which was nothing more than an elaborate series of digital switches. Once inside, Worm could manipulate the computer system.

Worm's short reach made Basilisk's plans a little more difficult. He had hoped they could conduct phase one from the comfort of Worm's lair. Instead they had been forced to break into the Goonhilly complex to directly access the computer system and satellite dish they needed.

Once Worm had got them inside, Basilisk was able to

All in a Day's Work

locate the dish that was channeling Internet traffic for Hero.com. Whether the station staff knew it or not, the heroes' Web site was transmitting its superpowers among ordinary Internet traffic, TV signals, and radio communications. Basilisk had even managed to locate the satellite that Hero.com used, off which it bounced its communications. Needless to say, there was no official log of such a satellite and Basilisk correctly assumed it had been launched in secret.

Basilisk had tried to explain to Worm that superpowers were stored in massive vats, donated by heroes, and more recently some had been artificially synthesized. Then through a complex process of quantum physics, they were digitized and transferred via the satellite, through the Internet, and into a person. The process relied on a constant "pulse" of information being broadcast directly to the superhero, without their knowledge, no matter where they were. The "pulse" was like a mobile phone signal. It was an instruction to the hero's body on how to use the power. If the body didn't get the message, then the power would become unstable and have, hopefully, terrible consequences. Villain.net worked on the same principle.

Under Basilisk's direction, Worm infiltrated the Hero.com satellite stream and interrupted it. It was only momentary, but it proved to Basilisk that it could be done.

"I do not see what help it is to us if we do not permanently break the signal from here," complained Worm as he pulled his hand from the computer terminal and sucked the sore tip of his finger.

"Because they will simply switch to another Ground Station."

"Then what have we just achieved? Nothing!"

Basilisk sighed. He felt like a teenager explaining simple technology to a confused parent. "We've just *proved* my plan will work. We can interrupt the signal. Any Downloaders using their powers would have felt the effect immediately. Now we need to overload the Hero.com Web site and temporarily stop it from functioning."

"Then we attack the Hero Foundation? Kill Courage?" Worm said with glee. He was an old foot soldier, not used to such tactical planning.

Basilisk fought to control his temper. They'd been through this almost every day.

"No. Our combined skills are not enough to bring the Foundation down."

"I think you underestimate me," Worm said with a hint of pride.

Basilisk looked long and hard at him. "No. No, I don't." A long moment passed before Worm processed the insult. He opened his mouth to retaliate, but Basilisk continued. "Remember, the Web site is just a weapon, a line of defense to stop the Foundation from being attacked. There are still the Primes, and the Foundation headquarters has its own internal electrical systems that need to be disabled."

"I have enough weapons to launch an assault—"

"Your weapons are so old that they fall apart when you pull the trigger!" snapped Basilisk. "Now we will temporarily overload the Web site with a virus. That will buy us time, and create enough of a diversion to make the Primes go into hiding. Then we implement phase two by recruiting a couple of other villains I have in mind. They will help us take out the Hero Foundation's satellite system."

"I don't understand."

Basilisk took a deep breath. Had it been anyone else, he would have been shouting at the top of his lungs. He at least had to pretend that he respected Worm.

"Remember, we want to use Hero.com to fight the Council. We don't want to destroy the Web site. We need to paralyze it long enough for us to bring down the Foundation's satellite. And then, even if their technicians get the Web site back up and running, they'll have no means of distributing the superpowers."

"Okay. I get it. I think."

"When we get to the satellite I'll be able to pinpoint the exact position of the Foundation's headquarters."

"And *then* we attack?"

"Yes. Phase three, we knock some heads together. They will have no heroes willing to lay their lives on the line to stop us."

"That I understand!" Worm was practically dancing with glee. If he achieved what Basilisk was promising, then he would have powers at his fingertips equal to the Council's. And if the plan failed, he still had Basilisk—dead or alive—to hand over to the Council instead. "Then what are we waiting for? Let's do it!"

"We've been waiting for your pea-sized brain to work out what the plan is," Basilisk mumbled under his breath as he pulled a slim USB memory stick from the depths of his cloak. He examined it as if it were a precious gem.

"Time to exercise your particular talent."

The computer virus on the USB stick was complex by any standards, and it had taken Basilisk the last few weeks to create it. He had swiped the basic structure from several nasty viruses that had recently stricken big businesses, combined with his working knowledge of Hero.com. He had a good knowledge of the hero Web site because he'd been one of the people who had helped steal it and convert it to Villain.net.

When he inserted the virus into the Ground Station system, it had been immediately isolated by the system's antiviral software. He needed Worm to bypass that.

Worm dipped his finger into the system. He closed

his eyes, visualizing the cyber world that his atoms were navigating through. He could "see" Basilisk's virus as a lump of electrons. He literally poked the malicious code past the security software and into the system. Only then could its devastating effects run free.

The virus pinged from the Ground Station to the Hero Foundation's private satellite, and then back down to the Foundation headquarters, where it buried itself in the HERO servers before sending a pulse of corrupted data outward.

The virus was subtle, just enough to trip the Foundation's computer systems, in the same way a power surge blows a fuse. As Foundation technicians rushed to try to fix the damage, the power surge slowly rippled through the satellite system in a destructive wave that would take hours to radiate out.

The next day brought stormy showers, which made Toby apprehensive. He was half-expecting Doc Tempest to smash through the windows and sweep him away. That thought, coupled with the memory of fighting Tempest in his ice base and seeing the super-fiend crushed under a block of ice, still haunted his dreams, even though it had been a while ago—one of his very first Hero missions. And now he had the smothering memory of nearly drowning to contend with.

All in all, Toby was beginning to worry that the superhero business was seriously stressing him out.

But today was a lazy Sunday, and he and Lorna had congratulated each other on successfully sneaking home exceptionally late during the night without their parents finding out. They hoped Pete and Emily had had the same good luck.

Walking down the stairs, Toby massaged his shoulder where the captain had hit him. Luckily he hadn't broken or dislocated it, but the skin sported a nasty purple-brown bruise that was tender to the touch. He turned into the living room—but found himself in the kitchen instead. They had moved to a new house after their old one was declared unsafe and demolished after Doc Tempest's attack. Toby liked the new house. It was a little bigger and still had that "new" smell. And right now it was filled with Christmas decorations that added to the excitement of the season.

He found Lorna in the living room with his mother and father, with a look on her face that warned him of what was happening. The television was on and his father was about to show them, yet again, video footage of his latest archaeology dig in Mexico.

John Wilkinson was a tall, thin man who always got excited over seemingly mundane things. Toby usually found him entertaining, but after watching the same

All in a Day's Work

footage *over and over*, the novelty had completely worn off.

Toby sat down next to his mother, Sarah, and offered a warm "good morning." Sarah returned his smile, and then exchanged pleasantly surprised looks with her husband. After the house had been struck by the tornado, she remembered nothing other than waking up in a field not far from home. But since then Toby had been incredibly civil toward her. He used to refuse a hug or any sign of affection, but now he did what she asked *almost* without question.

Toby had once thought his father was a closet super-hero rather than an archaeologist. But as it turned out there *wasn't* much more to his dad than met the eye.

"I just want to run through this again," said John Wilkinson excitedly. "I'm going to show it at the museum this evening before the public opening of my exhibition on Tuesday, so I need to keep it straight in my head."

He sat on his chair and looked around for the remote control, which he had a habit of always misplacing. Lorna glanced at Toby and shook her head. She buried herself in the broad pages of a glossy magazine, a world of celebrity gossip.

"Here we go," John exclaimed as he found the remote, which was tucked under his leg. Toby had been watching, out of the corner of his eye, the TV program that had been on. It was about the new Russian space shuttle

ferrying tourists into space from Kazakhstan. Both he and Lorna were desperate to try it, but at twenty million dollars it was just a little too expensive.

John hit the "play" button and the gleaming shuttle was replaced by shaky camcorder images of his archaeology dig. To Toby's untrained eyes it showed a mound of rubble among thick jungle.

"The jungle was so dense it took us two days to hack a narrow track through to the site," his father narrated. Then he suddenly looked up with a frown. "Do you think I should tell them about the trip home? Add a little more drama?"

"No, John," Sarah said firmly.

Again, Lorna peeked from behind her magazine and gave Toby a peculiar look.

John had cut the dig short to fly home after he had heard that a tornado had demolished his house and injured his wife. As the airplane was getting ready to land, the captain reported problems with the landing gear. John had panicked and called his wife on the in-flight phone, convinced they were going to crash. But something odd had happened minutes later as the aircraft circled the runway. John could have sworn he'd seen something *flying* alongside the plane. A minute later, the captain announced that the front wheel had now successfully extended and they could safely land.

Toby forced himself to watch the footage and listen

All in a Day's Work

to his father's increasingly excited narration as his team uncovered the tomb of some long-lost Mayan emperor. His father paced the room as he described the tension of opening the tomb, then lowered his voice to a whisper when he revealed that they had only examined the outer chamber before he was called away. The inner chamber still lay waiting for them to explore.

Toby stifled a yawn as the camera zoomed in on some symbols and murals on the wall. He had seen the ritualistic swirling icon so many times it had started to seep into his dreams, and his father's handheld camera work was beginning to make him feel nauseous. His dad might be a fantastic archaeologist, but he was a lousy cameraman—as all of their family photos proved.

The rest of the day passed in the inert stillness of an average Sunday. During the early evening Emily turned up and disappeared with Lorna into Lorna's room. Sarah and John left for the museum as Pete arrived. And a night without the parents snooping around meant a night to explore Hero.com.

Pete looked at Toby with a frown.

"Man, you look terrible."

"Thanks, Pete. I haven't been sleeping very well."

"Why?"

"Bad dreams. What about you? I mean, after everything we've been doing, doesn't it get to you?"

Pete shrugged and pushed past his friend. "Nah. If anything, I sleep better. More exercise than I'm used to!"

Pete made his way into the Wilkinsons' new office. It looked pretty much the same as the old one: it had not taken Toby's father long to give it that lived-in effect. Their old computer hard drive had been removed from Pete's computer and installed in a brand-new system that they had bought with the insurance money.

"The others here?" Pete asked as he sat down in front of the computer and booted it up.

Toby didn't answer right away. He had noticed that Pete's confidence had increased almost to the point of impoliteness since they had discovered the Web site.

"Do you mind?" Toby said, pointing to the chair. Pete looked startled for a second before he stood up and pulled over a free chair, mumbling, like old Pete.

"Course, sorry. Just getting excited. So where are they?"

"Right here," Emily said as she entered with Lorna. "Toby bossing you around again?"

"Yeah," Pete said with a laugh. Toby looked at him sideways; was it his imagination or was there a peeved tone to the laugh? Lorna and Emily pulled up chairs and didn't seem to notice.

"How you feeling after your swim yesterday?" Emily asked Toby with concern.

All in a Day's Work

"Shoulder's killing me and my ears still feel like I've got half the sea in them, but that'll go away eventually."

Emily squeezed his uninjured shoulder in a gesture of solidarity. Toby shifted uncomfortably, aware that Pete was giving him an odd look.

They didn't waste any time logging on to the Internet, and within a few seconds they were on Hero.com. Pete pressed a greasy finger on the screen.

"Look! Our 'Heroic score' has gone up!"

Sure enough, the points allotted by the Web site for each successful mission had increased, which was a good thing. If they failed the missions, then they would have to pay out of pocket to use the powers, until they'd built up enough credit through their successful deeds. At least the Heroism points meant they could download powers for free.

Toby had hoped to see a video message from Chameleon waiting for them on the site. He had spoken to him online a few times for advice. But he hadn't yet told the others that.

"Are we actually going to do another mission tonight?" Emily asked in a weary voice.

"What's up? Bored already?" goaded Pete.

"No. Tired. And we have school tomorrow."

"Great," Pete said without enthusiasm. "Dunno why they didn't just let us have Monday off."

It was an odd week for them. Tuesday and Wednesday

had been allocated as study days while the school was closed so that the woodworking department, which had mysteriously burned down a few weeks ago, could be demolished.

"Let's just look at the instruction manual then," Toby said.

"Exciting," Pete mumbled unenthusiastically.

Toby moved past several icons on the screen, none of which gave any obvious indication of what they represented. He stopped at one that depicted a wrench. The screen was replaced by reams of text that shimmered through numerous languages before settling on English. It did look like a technical manual, with icons and flow diagrams and simple illustrations.

Pete looked at him with a curious frown. "You found that pretty quickly."

When they had first met Chameleon, the shape-changing hero had expressed surprise that they hadn't read the Web site's instructions. Toby had searched through the site at the earliest opportunity and finally located it after several days of searching.

Pete shifted nervously in his chair. "So you've been on the site?"

"I wanted to read this."

"Been on it a lot?" Pete asked, probing for information.

Emily and Lorna exchanged a look. They knew

what Pete was getting at; he'd been subtly hinting at it for weeks.

"There's a lot to read," Toby said enthusiastically, oblivious to the edge in Pete's voice. He circled the mouse pointer around a section of the screen. "Like this section gives the basics of how the powers are transferred . . . " He trailed off when he became aware of the atmosphere in the room. Pete was staring hard at him. "What?"

"I'm just pointing out that you've been on *our* Web site a lot lately. Without *us*."

Toby groaned. "Come on, Pete. Don't start."

"Well, it's not fair that you have access to it but we don't. We found it together—"

"On *my* computer!"

"On Dad's computer," Lorna corrected him. Toby threw her an annoyed glance.

Pete thumped the desk. "*Your* computer? Is that how it is now?"

"I didn't mean—"

"We should all take turns at reviewing the Web site," Pete continued. "Or copy your hard drive so we all have it. It's just not fair that we have to go through you all the time."

"What's the point?" said Toby. "We're a team, we do things *together*."

"Exactly! That's my poi—"

A piercing feedback shriek from the computer's speakers drowned him out. At that exact moment the ceiling lights flickered and the monitor screen strobed through a rainbow of colors before it suddenly exploded in a supernova blast of light.

Infection

Thick fingers of electricity sprang from the monitor and raked across the floor and ceiling. Books shot off shelves and stacks of papers and cups of pens flew off the desk. Pete and Lorna toppled backward from their chairs, while Toby and Emily both pitched forward and hid under the desk as the light storm ravaged the office.

With a loud crack the lightning fizzled out. Toby peered cautiously over the desk. The room was awash with scattered papers, but luckily nothing seemed damaged; it was just as though a gust of wind had blown through the house.

Or a tornado had hit it, thought Toby darkly.

Pete checked his clothing; they had all been struck by the lightning but he could see no physical marks. He looked up to see the others staring at him with wide grins.

"Your hair!" giggled Emily. "It's sticking up everywhere!"

"*My* hair? You look pretty ridiculous too!"

Everybody's hair was standing on end, thin whispers of

smoke rising from each of them. Pete had mysteriously managed to get black smudges across his cheeks.

"What just happened?" he asked, standing up.

Emily brushed away the cordless phone that had fallen on her. "It felt like I was being tickled."

They looked at the screen. The Hero.com Web site was still there but a warning box had popped up on the screen:

"MALFUNCTION: Hero.com is temporarily off-line. Please try again later."

Pete pointed an accusing finger at Toby. "You broke it!"

"Don't be stupid."

"Then what happened?"

Toby found the wireless mouse halfway across the room and placed it back on the desk. He tried clicking on the icons but the computer just beeped stubbornly in response. Frustrated, he closed the browser. "Maybe it was a power surge? The site's been running sort of funny lately. Remember what happened yesterday?"

Pete huffed. "So we can't do anything?"

"We can always try again later," Toby said thoughtfully. "Should be working then. In the meantime we'd better clean up."

"Exciting," mumbled Pete.

"I got a new game for my Xbox. Afterward you can let me beat you at that."

Infection

The rest of the evening passed in relative peace. When they tried Hero.com later it was still down. That led Pete to speculate darkly over the fate of their heroic exploits.

Basilisk's mood was as dark as Pete's. When he got impatient he liked to pace briskly back and forth, since it made him seem imposing to his subordinates. Right now he wished he *could* pace through the forest clearing, but his injured leg wasn't regenerating. He resented the fact he had to prop himself up using a cane. Even though it was black carbon fiber, he still felt it made him look vulnerable.

He had been waiting for almost an hour in the pine forest clearing. The clouds threatened rain and he could see his own breath as he exhaled. He bitterly reflected that it was a far cry from his tropical paradise, which now lay in ruins after his first scheme to topple the Council of Evil had failed. And he felt angry that he was under the thumb of the bounty hunter. Of course, Worm was not around at the moment so he *could* simply walk away—but the pint-size villain would soon be on his tail. And he still needed Worm to carry out his plans. Basilisk was nothing if not resourceful. If things with Worm succeeded, then it would save Basilisk an awful lot of effort in executing it all on his own. And afterward he would deal with the diminutive Worm—he was a relic of the history books and didn't belong in a modern world.

A shriek in the forest snapped Basilisk from his ruminations. It was probably an owl. He looked across at the rogue he had recruited, who was leaning against a tree. Like him, she was a Prime—somebody who had the latent superpowers from birth, waiting for the chance to burst to life, usually in times of stress, or the old favorite: an industrial accident.

In her mid-twenties, she was tall and lithe with a tight white cowl over her head, her eyes visible through narrow slits. She pulled a stick of gum from the recesses of a cape that hung across her shoulders; no doubt keeping her warm, thought Basilisk as he shivered. When the woman moved, the cape seemed to possess a life of its own as it moved unnaturally, fluttering impossibly large behind her.

She was somebody Basilisk had known about for a couple of years, and it had only taken him a day to track her down and recruit her to their project. She was inspired partly by the cash Basilisk had promised, but more by the prospects of escaping from under the Council of Evil's yoke. Their constant meddling had made life a lot less fun for the younger villains.

She and Basilisk had been in the woods for several hours, waiting for Worm to meet them. She hadn't uttered a single word and had scowled at the nature

Infection

around her. She was a city girl. As the first drops of rain began to fall she finally opened her mouth, to complain about standing in the damp forest.

The art of conversation is truly dead, thought Basilisk, and he decided to respond with silence.

After a minute Basilisk felt the faintest of vibrations through his feet. They grew stronger by the second. Loose stones and rotting branches suddenly started to dance from the clearing as the earth trembled. Then a bronze machine rose from the ground at an angle. About the size of a bus, it also had gnashing blades that consumed dirt, branches, and foliage.

Basilisk watched as the sleek vehicle pulled itself from the dirt on hundreds of articulated spikes mounted across the fuselage, designed to pull the machine through the earth. The front was nothing more than a gaping hole with circular teeth that chewed the soil, carried it through a tube that ran the length of the craft, and deposited it at the rear. It was a simple system that allowed the machine to move underground without leaving a tunnel or even a trace it had passed by. Two large green glass windows at the front made it resemble a bug, and the fins on the side were a stylistic remnant of the 1930s, when the machine was built.

A portal hissed open and Worm stepped out with a grin. "My old ship! The *Nematode*. She still works, after all these years!"

Basilisk poked and prodded it like a professional mechanic. "I've only seen photos of this thing. I could have used this a few weeks ago."

The woman scrutinized the machine doubtfully. "It belongs in a museum . . . or a junkyard."

Worm returned the skeptical look. "Ah, I assume you must be the cat burglar?"

"They call me Trojan," replied the woman in a gentle Southern accent and with a humorless smile. "And I prefer *'escape artiste.'* I heard about you too, Grandpa. Thought you were dead?"

"A thief's a thief," snapped Worm pompously. "And in my day, women had a more civil tone of voice when they spoke to their elders and superiors."

"Times change, Gramps. This is *my* day now." She walked the length of the ship, examining it with a critical eye.

Worm refrained from snapping a retort. Instead he turned back to Basilisk. "And you believe this *riffraff* can aid our ambitious plan?"

"Indeed she can," said Basilisk. "Her skills are second to none. But we need one more."

"And you?" asked Worm, casting a shrewd eye on Basilisk. "This plan of yours is all that's preventing me from handing you over to the Council and claiming the bounty. I fail to see your contribution."

Basilisk's eyes flared neon blue, and even though

Infection

Worm could not see under the dark hood, he knew the villain was grinning.

"Me? I'm the mastermind. Without me there would be no plan. And at the very least, I'm the one who is protecting you from being torn apart by Trojan. She's a lot stronger than she looks, and I don't think you two got off to a very good start."

Worm flicked a worried glance at Trojan. Although she was thin, he couldn't shake the fact that she could indeed kill him if provoked. *How times have changed*, thought Worm. There was a time when other villains feared *him*.

Basilisk rapped a hand against the bronze hull. "Your ship is archaic. Perhaps we need something more . . . modern?"

Worm looked surprised. "The *Nematode* is state-of-the-art. . . . Well, it used to be."

Basilisk waved to Trojan. "Let's go. This bucket of bolts will get us to our next step at least."

"Where are we going?" asked Worm, who was starting to feel Basilisk had a little too much authority for a prisoner on reprieve.

"To hell," Basilisk said with a chuckle.

School had improved noticeably over the last couple of weeks, Pete thought. Even when he hadn't downloaded superpowers, he was feeling much more confident. That could also be attributed to the fact that Jake Hunter and his gang of thugs hadn't been at school for a while.

But today saw the return of Big Tony and Knuckles, who were walking to school deep in conversation, although Pete couldn't imagine any conversation between the two of them lasting for long, or not containing profanities instead of the more normal adjectives.

Pete trailed behind them, knowing that overtaking them would risk him becoming a target. After a few minutes it was obvious something was amiss as the two bullies were keeping unusually low profiles, as though not wanting to attract attention.

When a kid in a year below Pete, who was another firm bullying favorite, stepped from a side street and straight into the thugs' path, they didn't bat an eyelid. The kid ran away as quickly as possible, unscathed.

It was then that Pete registered that the other two members of their single-digit IQ posse were missing: Scuffer and the leader of the herd, Jake Hunter. Pete smiled; that could only be a good thing.

Pete had an increasingly irritating day. Aside from the mounting homework for them to do over the next two days' "vacation," he couldn't find Toby, Emily, or Lorna at break. A paranoid thought suggested that they were all enjoying Hero.com together. He ignored it. He trusted Emily and Lorna more than Toby. He was certain they wouldn't cheat behind his back. Then again he did feel a tremor of jealousy that Emily and Toby seemed a little closer than usual. Or was that just another twinge of paranoia?

Feeling confused and alone, he headed for the sanctuary of the bathroom. He was there when the bell rang and he had to sprint to his English class. The school yard was empty by the time Pete ran across it—and into the path of Knuckles and Big Tony quickly leaving the science wing.

Knuckles stared at him with a scowl. "Watch what ya doin', Professor. You wanna broken arm?"

Pete's mouth was dry. He'd faced armed thieves, smugglers, and a weather-controlling supervillain. But without the comfort of his superpowers he suddenly felt vulnerable.

Big Tony pulled on his companion's sleeve. "Knock it off, Knucks. We've got a . . . er . . . class . . . remember?" He jerked a thumb across the yard.

To Pete's amazement Knuckles backed off and they hurried across the yard without another glance. From bitter experience Pete knew he should at least have gotten a numbing punch in the arm.

Mr. Rush gave Pete a stern glance when he ran into the classroom.

"Ah, Peter Kendall. Good of you to take time from your busy schedule to join us."

Snickers of laughter rippled across the room.

"Sorry, sir. I was—"

"Out saving the world, I would imagine. Now sit down, we have a lot to get through today. I've teamed you up in pairs. You're with Miss Forshaw."

Pete glanced at Toby, who had been paired with a cute Asian girl. Pete reluctantly moved to his seat next to a girl who was almost twice his size and scared him almost as much as Knuckles did.

The lesson crawled along as Mr. Rush extolled the virtues of the book they were being forced to read. Pete had been told it was a classic, but he couldn't see why. Nothing happened and all the characters spoke in an old-fashioned way. But he dutifully took notes as the teacher tried to explain *why* the story was so important.

A slight noise made Pete glance up and he saw Toby had knocked his pen off the desk. Either that or the pen had tried to commit suicide out of boredom. Toby reached down, and his arm extended by half its length so that he could comfortably pick up the pen. His arm looked as though it was made from rubber.

Pete watched, stunned. Toby stared at his arm, which had now shrunk back to normal. He quickly looked around the room to check that nobody had seen that display of inhuman power. No one paid him any attention. When he noticed Pete staring dumbly at him it seemed, to Pete at least, he *tried* to act surprised and mouthed the word, "Wow!"

Pete felt crushed. His suspicions had been confirmed: Toby had been downloading superpowers without the rest of them knowing. Toby and Lorna fought for days when she had suggested that they should let the world know about their abilities and cash in on the fame. Pete had sided with her; fame certainly meant money. And right now his family was penniless. But Toby had taken the moral high ground, telling them all to act responsibly.

The traitor!

Pete didn't listen for the rest of the class. His mind was elsewhere as he stared at the words in the book. He thought about how he was going to confront Toby. He felt sick from the betrayal.

Pete shot up a hand. "Sir—I feel sick!"

He didn't wait for permission, but ran from the class-room holding his stomach.

The corridors were mercifully empty as Pete ran down them. The queasy feeling in his stomach had ebbed the moment he left class. He exited the block and walked out into the teachers' parking lot, where he leaned against the wall to catch his breath.

Why would Toby lie?

A sudden thump startled him as the door he'd come through was kicked open and hit the wall with force. Knuckles and Big Tony sprinted out wearing frightened expressions. They froze when they caught sight of Pete and looked wildly around before accepting that he wasn't a threat. Then their panic changed to a predatory gaze.

A quick glance around the empty parking lot confirmed that Pete was trapped and alone. Big Tony nervously glanced back the way they had come.

"Coast's clear," he said.

Knuckles composed himself. Deliberately stretched his neck from one side to the other with a horrible crack, and then popped the knuckles on both his fists.

"How's it going, Prof?" he said, advancing a step. "Shouldn't you be in class, like a good brainiac?"

Pete's eyes darted side to side as he looked for an exit. He felt the words tumbling out before he could stop them. "Shouldn't you both be back in remedial class?"

"What?" screamed Knuckles, his skin flushing like a beet. "You little nerd! I'm going to smash your face in for that!"

Pete saw the fist being clenched and raised toward him. He closed his eyes in anticipation and waited for it to connect. It seemed like an age had passed and yet he still felt nothing. He opened his eyes, wondering if something had scared Knuckles away—but no, in

Infection

reality only a second had passed and he saw a close-up of Knuckles's fist connecting with his nose.

The pain was unbearable. Multicolored lights flashed before Pete's eyes. He fell to the ground with the peculiar salty smell of his own blood oozing from his nose. His cheap glasses spun off and landed a few feet away.

Knuckles laughed loudly as he stared down at Pete, who had one hand across his nose, the other patting the ground to retrieve his glasses.

Big Tony gave his friend a high five. "Nice one."

Knuckles felt elated. Professor had gone down without a fight, which is *exactly* how he wanted it. The quicker they fell, the harder he looked. But his smile slowly drifted, his mouth sagging open.

Pete's nose shifted under its own volition and they all heard a loud snap as the cartilage realigned itself. The swelling around his face deflated like a burst balloon, and the bleeding stopped in an instant.

Pete shoved his glasses back on and felt his strength return in a huge wave that coursed through his body. He sprang to his feet, suddenly full of energy and feeling *very* angry.

"That's the last time you hit me!" he roared.

Without thinking, he balled up his tiny fist and threw a punch at Knuckles's stomach. In an ordinary fight he would have missed the bully, or if he'd been fortunate enough to connect, the punch would have felt like a tap.

But this wasn't an ordinary fight.

Pete saw his hand expand to double its normal size, and it shimmered with a faint blue aura. When it connected with Knuckles, the bully felt as if a bomb had detonated in his stomach.

The breath was expelled from him and he heard a couple of ribs crack. The punch was so strong that Knuckles was lifted clean off his feet and propelled more than thirty feet across the parking lot. He bounced off a MINI Cooper, crumpling the hood, ricocheted off a Ford, denting the roof and shattering the windows, before finally slamming to a halt against the side of a Honda, smashing in the entire door panel as though it had been struck by another car. A cacophony of car alarms sounded, and the Honda's airbag abruptly expanded.

Knuckles let out a long groan, indicating he was still alive. Pete swiveled around to face Big Tony, who was as white as a sheet.

"You're one of *them*! You're a *freak*! Get away from me!"

Big Tony tripped over his own feet as he fled, distancing himself from Pete and not at all concerned about his friend's condition. Pete stared at his hand, which was still double its size; veins throbbed under the bluish skin. He shook it, the action returning his limb to normal.

"I've got powers?" he mumbled under his breath. "How's that possible?"

A voice bellowed from a window above Pete—the unmistakable tones of the school principal, Mr. Harris.

"What's going on out there?"

Pete pressed himself flat against the wall. If he were caught in this mess, he didn't think he could explain his way out of it. A quick glance at Knuckles confirmed that he wasn't going anywhere soon. Pete ducked back into the school and ran for the bathroom, fervently hoping he wouldn't bump into anybody on his way.

It was not just the boys who were experiencing erratic surges of superpowers. Emily had been slogging through a cross-country run during PE when her legs became a blur and she rocketed toward the finish line in the blink of an eye. Luckily it all happened so quickly that nobody had actually *seen* her move; the other students had been staring exhaustedly at their own feet.

The experience rattled her, and with shaking legs she moved as slowly as possible back to the locker room, although it seemed the power had vanished just as suddenly as it had appeared.

Lorna, who was in most of the same classes as Emily, had avoided running around in the cold by volunteering to help put together an art installation in the hall. The art teacher, Mrs. Skinner, had left her and another girl, Mary Sommers, to put up the display boards. Lorna glowered at Mary, who not only seemed to outperform Lorna in every subject, but also received more attention from the boys than she did. And of course, it was always the *same* boys that she liked. Mary was explaining how much better her display layout would be from the art room and dragging the boards into position.

Lorna was so furious she burst into flames.

Orange waves of fire consumed her body, just like the inferno that she had seen cover Pete the day they first stumbled upon the Web site. It felt like taking a dip in a pleasantly warm bath—but the fierce flames scorched the fabric display boards next to her, leaving them black and charred.

The flames extinguished with a dull whump seconds later, leaving Lorna and her clothes in one piece—just as Mary poked her head out from the art room. She immediately noticed the burn marks.

"What happened?" she asked with a frown.

Lorna was speechless. She spun on her heels and ran down the hall, leaving Mary Sommers shouting for her to come back and help. Lorna ran through a second set

Infection

of doors before she stopped at the staircase and quickly examined her hands. They seemed okay. Then she was distracted by a banging noise.

"What was that?" she asked aloud.

She was answered by a clang, like a table toppling over. It came from the floor below, from a basement room, which the students were banned from entering but occasionally did on a dare. It was dark down there and there were rumors of a ghostly presence. Lorna knew the janitor stored extra chairs and tables down there. Perhaps it was him? She peered over the rail.

The lights were off, so it probably wasn't the janitor, right? There were the faint sounds of movement. There was definitely *somebody* down there.

"Hello?"

Curious, she descended, her footsteps echoing. Then she saw movement in the shadows, and heard a familiar voice.

"Hello, Lorna."

At lunch Pete and Toby stayed as far away from the other students as possible. Toby didn't know what was bothering Pete, and he wandered over to find out.

"You saw what happened to me in class?"

"Yeah. I thought you'd been downloading powers on the sly without us."

Toby shook his head. "I didn't. It just happened. I didn't even think about it!"

"You swear you didn't?" Pete had no doubt what happened today had nothing to do with Toby, but he was still suspicious that his friend had used the Web site in the past without telling him. Now was as good a time as any to catch him in a lie.

"Why would I do that? I've only been on the site to read the manual, which goes on forever. And I've talked to Chameleon a few times, but I haven't done *anything* else. I swear it!"

"Just seems suspicious, you spontaneously developing superpowers," sniffed Pete, playing the innocent card as much as possible.

Toby looked at him levelly. "What can I say? I was as surprised as you. We've been friends for years, I thought you trusted me?"

Pete held his gaze for a few seconds before he crumbled and a smile twitched at his mouth. "Sure. Same thing happened to me."

"What? You knew all along?" Toby snapped.

Pete ignored the tone; he was too excited to explain how he had dealt with Knuckles. In the middle of his flamboyant description of fleeing the scene of the crime and avoiding capture by Mr. Harris, Toby noticed Emily approaching.

"Here's Em," said Toby, giving her a wave.

Infection

"She's got her own superpowers. She can find us any-where," said Pete.

"She always seems to be able to find *you*," Toby quipped, repressing a smile. Pete frowned at him and was about to reply, but Toby cut him off.

"Hi, Em." The look on her face told him everything he needed to know. "Let me guess: something weird just happened?"

Emily looked at him in surprise before nodding. "You too?"

"Both of us. Here comes Lorna."

"Lorn, what kept you?" Emily asked.

Lorna looked flushed, and stammered her words. "Nothing. I was just in the basement, and I . . . er . . . "

"Basement?" said Emily, studying her friend.

"You had powers misfiring?" asked Toby.

Lorna composed herself. "I take it that means we all did?"

"The Web site went bananas last night, and now this? Something's gone seriously wrong," Toby said. "I wonder if we'll get them again, or if it was a onetime thing?"

"Gone wrong?" said Emily, who was still looking oddly at Lorna. "I don't want powers that go off at random. It's too dangerous. We're all lucky nobody saw what happened. We might not be so fortunate next time."

"Could be a virus," commented Pete. "Computers get them all the time. And if your anti-spyware's not up-to-date, then something could've clashed and—bang!—superpowers downloading all over the place."

"We have the right software. Up-to-date too."

"Yeah, but do *they* have one?" Pete's expression suddenly turned thoughtful. "If we have powers and the site's no longer working, then do you think they're permanent?"

"No chance. We're not Primes. They'll wear off . . . at some point."

"Maybe we are Primes?" Pete said thoughtfully. "Primes are born with powers, but they don't know they have them, right? Not until something triggers them."

Lorna's eyes went wide. "You may be right."

Toby shook his head. "No he's not."

"Typical you'd say that," Pete shot back. Toby was surprised at the harsh tone in his voice. "Always trying to stop us from doing what *we* want. But what's stopping us from going public with our powers now? Make some money from all this. If we have them and nobody else can access the site, then we've got nothing to hide."

Lorna brightened. "We could get on talk shows!"

Toby held up his hands in an attempt to calm them down. "No way. We talked about this."

"No, *you* talked. We listened," Lorna said with an

Infection

edge to her voice. "We're the ones going out and taking the risks all the time. And what do we get for it? The stupid Web site telling us to keep quiet all the time."

Pete nodded in agreement. "And now it looks like we have powers without having to download them. I think that makes us special."

Lorna nodded in agreement. "Totally!"

Their voices were rising, and Toby had to quickly look around to make sure they had not been overheard. He noticed Emily was keeping quiet, no doubt reluctant to argue against Pete and Lorna. "But our powers do good. They fight evil. I know it sounds silly, but we make the world a better place. We are trusted to keep this quiet. And if something's wrong, then we have a responsibility to find out why and try to help!"

"I couldn't agree more," said a new voice that made them all turn in alarm. A tall man was standing close by with his hands clasped together. He studied them with a slight smile. He wore thin square-rimmed glasses with thick black frames that complemented his impeccably sharp black suit, pristine white shirt, and narrow black tie.

"Who are you?" Toby said in a firm, but low, voice.

"Oh, you can speak up," said the man, gesturing around the yard. "They can't hear you."

Toby looked around. Everything seemed normal, and he could hear the constant background screams of the yard. A football rolled over, and an elementary school kid scrambled to retrieve it. It bounced off of Pete's leg.

"Watch it!" scolded Pete.

The boy was standing right next to them and scooped up the ball with a puzzled frown. His eyes moved across the group but didn't focus on anything. With a shrug the boy returned to his friends.

"You made us invisible!" Pete accused.

"Not invisible," said the man, as though he was discussing the weather. "Just temporarily imperceptible. They can see us perfectly, but their brains choose not to register that fact. Out of the corner of their eyes they can see us just fine, but when they turn to look, their brains just filter us out. It's all very . . . *quantum*."

"You never answered my question," said Toby. "Who are you?"

The man smiled, although there was no humor involved in the process. His gray eyes studied Toby shrewdly. "You must be Toby Wilkinson. Yes, yes . . . the makings of a leader. If only you could keep your team in line."

"We're not *his* team," muttered Pete, but the man didn't acknowledge him. Instead he kept his gaze on Toby.

"I am the person to call when you have something that needs concealing or a problem that needs resolving."

Something clicked at the back of Pete's mind. Stacks

of useless knowledge from films, comic books, and science fiction stories brimmed in his head.

"Men in Black!" he exclaimed. "You're one of them!"

Emily laughed derisively. "Now you're getting mixed up with movies!"

"No," Pete said firmly. "In real life they're supposed to intimidate people who think they've seen flying saucers or things they shouldn't have."

"He is right," the man said solemnly, wiping the grin off Emily's face. "I am one of many *fixers*, and that name has been applied to us. It is a sad sign of the times that when you dress smartly, you get singled out from the crowd. Think of me as a lawyer."

Emily's parents were lawyers, so she felt on familiar ground. "Then who are you working for?"

"The same side as you. Please come with me and I shall explain." He gestured to a black SUV that was parked next to the school gates. The parking lot was milling with teachers and police who were inspecting the damage caused by Pete's assault on Knuckles, but none of them paid the slightest attention to the car that was parked in a no-parking zone.

"If you're worrying about accepting a ride from a stranger, I assure you, you're quite safe."

Lorna offered a terse smile. "I didn't think that *we* were the ones at risk. You're the one climbing into a car with four lethal superheroes."

The man glanced at the wreckage in the parking lot, then back to Lorna. His face was deadly serious. "So I see. Then I hope I can trust you?"

The back of the SUV was comfortable and easily accommodated the five of them. The seats were oriented to face one another, and only as the man slid the door closed behind them did Toby become aware that there was a driver behind the tinted partition. The vehicle swayed gently, betraying that they were in motion.

"Where are we going?" Toby asked sharply.

"There is not a moment to lose, so I thought it better to talk on the move."

Toby looked at his friends. Emily was unreadable, but she never took her eyes from the man, and her fingers flexed as though she was ready to incinerate him at a moment's notice. Lorna shrugged and sat back in the seat. Pete folded his arms. "You're apparently the team leader, dude."

The man unhinged a flat monitor from the ceiling and swiveled it around to face them.

"I assume you would want to hear this from somebody you trust."

An image flickered on the screen, and Chameleon appeared—in his natural guise of a handsome twenty-year-old. He was paler than usual, emphasized by his jet-black hair that came to a widow's peak. A scar ran across his face that hadn't been there the last time Pete had seen him.

"Greetings, heroes." Chameleon's voice was strained and wary. "This is a recorded message. Please forgive this unorthodox approach but we are facing desperate times and the Foundation has tasked me with the capture of a deadly supervillain: the Hunter. You can trust Mr. Grimm here. He will explain the situation and I hope we can count on your support. Good luck."

The image flicked to black.

"That just about explains everything," Pete said sarcastically.

Mr. Grimm was undeterred by Pete. "I have been hired by the Higher Energy Research Organization to track you down."

"Er . . . who and how?" said Pete.

"The Hero Foundation. You know, the people who gave you all those nice superpowers that you have been playing around with?"

"Hero? I thought that's what we were, not *who* we were working for!" exclaimed Pete.

"Being a hero is a state of mind, not simply a power you download from the Internet. Even a criminal has that ability."

Pete sat back in his chair and couldn't shake the

feeling that Mr. Grimm was a personality combination of every teacher he disliked.

Mr. Grimm gazed at Toby as he spoke. "The Hero.com Web site has been sabotaged. Initially the main global feed was disrupted, hence your powers behaving erratically when you were out on a mission. Then a computer virus was introduced into the system. Inserted directly into the Ground Station pipeline so it bypassed the firewalls and viral scanners. It was a real piece of craftsmanship. Metamorphic coding, the likes of which we have not seen before. It created strange loops and even held genetic modification algorithms that—" He hesitated, suddenly aware of the blank faces looking at him.

"So . . . it was bad?" Toby said, summarizing the words he did understand.

"Crippling," Mr. Grimm responded, regaining his composure. "It took almost twenty-four hours to spread, but when it did it created a biofeedback. Er . . . the pretty fireworks that shot from your computer screen." It was obvious Mr. Grimm was not used to speaking to children, and this made Lorna increasingly dislike the man's emotionless countenance.

"So it was some kind of feedback that hit us?" she asked. "And you mentioned genetic modification—do you mean the way Hero.com alters our bodies and gives us superpowers?"

Infection

Mr. Grimm's eyebrow trembled a fraction, the only sign that he was impressed.

"Indeed. It so happened that you four were the only people logged on to the site at the time. Other Downloaders around the globe had already deployed their hyper energy . . . uh . . . superpowers, beforehand, which have since expired. Others tried after the site went down and were unsuccessful."

Pete frowned. The leather seat creaked as he leaned forward. "So, logically . . . we're the only heroes with superpowers?"

Mr. Grimm fixed his steely gaze on Pete.

"Indeed. That is why *everything* is now hanging on your decisions. You are the only heroes left."

Breakout

Stunned silence greeted Mr. Grimm's comment. Toby was the first to speak up.

"That's impossible. What about Chameleon, or even you? You're both Primes, right? We can't be the only people with powers!"

Mr. Grimm steepled his fingers under his chin. "Remember what I said. Being a hero is a state of mind. There are fewer Primes than ever before. There was once a theory that Primes were the next step in human evolution. Something new. But alas, history bred more Primes than there are now. Multiple theories have been offered: climate change, artificial preservatives in foods, chemicals used to purify drinking water. You name it and somebody has had a theory about it. But the fact is we do not know why. Those Primes that are born and discover their gifts are increasingly becoming, how can I say this—influenced by acquisitive motivations."

Emily thought about that for a moment. "You mean they become villains?"

"Yes. I suppose 'criminals' is a more precise term. Even

those who are not seeking global domination, the good guys, are ushered into the shadows as their numbers dwindle. Destined to keep a low profile for fear of becoming extinct. The days are gone when a Prime will fight for what he believes in—they are not heroes, they are just people gifted with powers. That's why we have Hero.com, to make real heroes when those who have the power are too afraid to wield it. Without Hero.com, the Hero Foundation is just another organization that will crumble to ashes, and humanity will be faced with an army of supervillains that they have no hope of defeating."

Everybody swapped glances. This was certainly not how they had imagined superhero life. A dying breed? Extinction? Mr. Grimm had not answered anything, but had simply provoked more questions. Toby voiced this.

"Good," replied the man in black. "Questions are healthy. The pursuit of knowledge is a heroic cause, is it not?"

Pete clicked his fingers and felt smug that he had assembled the jigsaw pieces before the others. But the picture was not looking very appealing.

"That's why they created Hero.com—to give out powers to people who didn't have any, so the heroic Primes wouldn't be forced into the open. They wouldn't be targets for the bad guys."

"An excellent deduction. The scientific accumulation of Prime powers was a project started under the banner of the Higher Energy Research Organization, headed by the world's top minds. They succeeded in distilling and even replicating their superpowers through genetic research. It was a small step from that to being able to incubate the raw power and then apply it to an ordinary human. The digital interface of the Web site is simply a method of quantum tunneling the genetic information into your body. It's all very complicated. But the Web site keeps sending instructional pulses out to your body. When the pulses stop, the powers fade. Somehow the pulse packed your bodies with more powers than we would safely administer. That's why they're unstable, and wearing off at erratic rates."

Toby's brow was creased in concentration. "I kind of get it."

Mr. Grimm flashed a rare smile. "Like I said, it's all very *quantum*."

Something was bothering Emily. "But why do we have powers now? We didn't download anything."

"An unexpected side effect from the virus attack. As you were the only ones online, you took the full hit of the feedback. Dozens, possibly hundreds, of powers struck you simultaneously. We have no idea what they are, how long they will last, or how you can control them.

Breakout

But the hypothesis is that you have absorbed enough energy to last the week. That should be enough time."

"For what exactly?" Toby asked warily.

"To help defend the Hero Foundation."

"So just a small job then?" said Pete sarcastically.

"You can start by tracking down the culprits who sabotaged Hero.com and stop them before they launch a full-scale attack on the Foundation. Even now we have technicians working to bring the site back online, but that could take a while; the viral damage was extensive. As long as Hero.com is off-line, the Hero Foundation, and the world, is vulnerable."

"So do I have this right?" Pete asked. "We go out and risk our necks to save a bunch of superheroes, like you, who are cowering away in case the big bad villains hurt you?"

Mr. Grimm's eyes narrowed a fraction. "I would have put it more eloquently. But you are correct. We are too valuable to risk."

"And we're expendable?" barked Lorna.

"You have proven yourselves as heroes already. You have risked your lives on several tasks—from fighting Doc Tempest to stopping more mundane petty crimes. But each act, from stopping a bully to destroying those pirates, has huge implications on the world."

Lorna was not convinced. "That was different! Those stupid little jobs Toby chose didn't change anything. So what if a boat full of pirated DVDs gets through? Some film companies lose money. Hardly a crime."

Mr. Grimm thought for a moment. "Have you heard of the butterfly effect? It's a quantum thing."

Lorna sat back in confusion. "Now you're changing the subject."

"In London a butterfly flaps its wings, which in turn displaces air particles. Those particles hit other particles, bouncing like a pinball. One air particle hits two air particles. Now those two particles hit another two particles. Now we have four, which hit another four to make eight. Then sixteen . . . then thirty-two. The number of air particles displaced grows exponentially. In other words, by the time air particles have bounced off one another halfway around the globe the number of displaced particles has grown to thousands of billions. Enough, for example, to cause a cyclone that could devastate China."

"That's one lethal butterfly!" murmured Pete. "They should just kill it."

Emily's brow was creased in concentration. "So one tiny action can have bigger consequences?"

"The pirated films would have been sold, the money passed to the organized gangs who then buy weapons with which they cause acts of terrorism—which results in the loss of lives. By stopping that freighter you have possibly saved the lives of hundreds of people."

Breakout

"Okay, I understand now," said Lorna. "But that still doesn't make us expendable."

"You stopped that boat because you thought you were doing some good. Now you are being asked to help stop a catastrophe. There are more criminal Primes than law-abiding ones. Hero.com was created to address that problem. We can't create more Primes, but we can create new heroes. Without help from other heroes, Primes are forced to hide or risk extinction. There are exceptions, a handful of Primes who are risking themselves. I am one, Chameleon is another."

"So why don't *you* stop the bad guys then?" Pete demanded. He was feeling angry about being thought of as expendable. That comment summed up his life.

"A fair point. We are busy protecting the public, trying to stop the other villains out there who are using the situation to their advantage. That would cause total anarchy and alert the public to our existence."

"Is that so bad?" asked Lorna. "The second part, I mean."

"Supers have remained out of the public eye for centuries. No good could come of the world knowing our secret now. People like routine and the belief that their leaders are in control. They would find the truth too . . . disturbing."

Silence filled the car as the friends thought about the situation they were in.

Toby nodded. His decision was made. "Okay. We'll do it."

Lorna looked at him in astonishment. "*We* will?"

"Come on, Lorn. This is a real chance to help."

"He's right," said Emily. Toby was surprised at his ally. He looked at Pete, who shrugged back.

"I still think we should be getting paid real money to do this. But okay. Let's save the day. Again."

Lorna exhaled loudly. "Okay, while you real super-heroes cower away in your hideouts, what are we supposed to do?"

Mr. Grimm gave her a polite nod. "So you are all in. Perfect. It appears that there are two villains behind this plot. They intend to recruit others to their cause of bringing down the Hero Foundation. They have recruited one already, Trojan. We suspect they will try to free an inmate in Diablo Island Penitentiary next—someone who would be perfect for their cause."

"A prison?" asked Pete.

"A very secure prison for supervillains, and the occasional hero who crosses to the wrong side of the law."

"So who is it they want?"

"A very lethal customer with a unique talent. If we can stop our suspects before they try to release the prisoner, then this whole affair will be quickly quashed." Mr. Grimm met their gazes in turn. "Everything depends upon your success."

Breakout

Pete shattered the solemnity of the moment.

"So. No pressure then?"

"How do we get to this Diablo Island?" Emily asked.

"You fly, of course," Mr. Grimm replied.

"Cool, so we definitely have flying powers?" said Pete with a grin.

"No. I meant: you fly."

Pete was suddenly aware that the SUV had stopped. Mr. Grimm opened the door. They were in the middle of the countryside, parked on a dirt track. Sitting in a field was a black Bell/Agusta tilt-rotor aircraft—the massive helicopter-style wings were already whirling. Once in flight the rotors would swivel forward like a traditional aircraft. It was the ultimate in luxury transportation.

"Oh," said Pete, feeling somewhat disappointed. "You meant fly like *that*."

Huge storm-surge waves pounded the shore, soaking the bronze *Nematode*, which had surfaced atop a cliff. An abandoned church stood close by, the rusting bell adding a mournful note to the strong winds.

Inside the craft, Worm, Basilisk, and Trojan peered through the curved canopy at Diablo Island offshore, almost lost in the curtain of rain. They were off the coast of Iceland, in a spot chosen because its constant foul weather made any air assault difficult. The island was composed almost entirely of iron rock that made Worm's superpowered transportation skills impotent and would probably damage the *Nematode* if it tried to dig through.

The walls of the prison were attached snugly to the cliff edge and sloped outward in a V-shape so that if any daring rescuer managed to scale the cliff, they would then be faced with a one-hundred-foot, smooth titanium-coated wall that overhung the jagged rocks below. The wall was topped by an assortment of advanced sensors and surveillance cameras, and the interior was bathed in bright floodlights that ensured it was as bright as midday throughout the long Arctic nights. In short, it was one of the most impregnable places on earth.

However, it looked as if somebody had managed to break out.

The *Nematode*'s observation windows magnified their target like a set of giant binoculars. "Lens magnifiers! My own design." Worm beamed proudly, but his companions didn't seem at all impressed.

"It may have been state-of-the-art a hundred years ago, Gramps," said Trojan with a sly smile. "These days we'd use a camera."

Basilisk stared hard at the island. "There is no bank vault more tightly guarded."

A large hole had been melted through one of the walls

and construction teams were in the process of patching it up, watched over by an entire platoon of tough-looking armed guards—Enforcers: a secret army created and funded by the United Nations and dedicated to keeping supervillains in check.

"Looks like we may be too late," quipped Worm. "Your boy may have already fled."

"Escape is supposed to be impossible," said Basilisk, never taking his eyes from the island.

"Escape *was* supposed to be impossible," said Trojan. "It was some new guy they had in there. You guys aren't very clued in to current events, huh? Very uncool. How're you supposed to know what's going on in the world around you?"

"Worm's television is a couple of decades out-of-date," muttered Basilisk.

"They're calling him the Hunter. There's a big search on apparently."

Unease crept over Basilisk—and for somebody whose gaze can turn a man to stone, that was a rare occurrence.

"The Hunter? Who is he?"

Trojan shrugged and turned away from the magnified screen. It was starting to give her a headache. "Dunno. Some newbie hotshot. Course they're all saying how impossible escape is. But I don't believe anything's impossible. I've yet to come across somewhere *really* impregnable."

If the Hunter was who he thought, then Basilisk would have to watch his back from now on.

Worm looked away and rubbed his eyes. "So how do we get in now that the guard has doubled?"

Basilisk composed himself and extended a hand toward Trojan. "There are very few places in the universe that Trojan can't walk right into. And she's taking us along too."

The aircraft rocked as it hit a pocket of turbulence. Emily gripped the overhead luggage compartment for support. She was returning from the bathroom, where she had changed from her school clothes into the plain black canvas pants and black thermal jacket they had all been given.

"More appropriate hero attire," Mr. Grimm had said.

Their benefactor had shown them a presentation highlighting what was known about Basilisk, Worm, and Trojan. They had watched a video about Diablo Island. It reminded Toby of some kind of elaborate commercial with swelling music and a narrator who spoke every line with a sense of awe. But in a nutshell they had learned all about the Enforcers and the island prison that had been built to contain supervillains.

Toby realized they hadn't even begun to scratch the surface of the amazing new world they were immersed in. Pete was oddly quiet, but at least Lorna had brightened up when they were offered some fruit to eat during the flight. She polished off almost the entire bowl.

Even though the main site was off-line, Mr. Grimm had been able to access Hero.com's RSS news feed, or Really Simple Syndication—news headlines that are common across most Web sites and displayed the latest news and gossip. The headlines described the aftermath of the Hunter's escape from the island.

They were all given a small mobile-phone-size wristband, with a touch screen on top. Mr. Grimm explained that it would attempt to control the energy storm that was rampaging through their bodies at the moment. He warned them that it was experimental technology and not one hundred percent reliable, but it should allow them to use the powers they had inadvertently downloaded. Although without the control pulse from the Hero.com Web site, there would be no telling just how long the powers would last or exactly how controllable they would be.

Mr. Grimm indicated a small touch screen with a single button. It was a teleport power that was stored in the device. He tapped a transparent cylinder on the side of the casing. A brownish liquid sloshed around.

"That's a raw superpower?" Pete asked, amazed.

"Yes, an artificially created power," said Mr. Grimm.

"Looks like sewage."

"It's just strong enough to get you back home. It's already been preprogrammed so you don't have to visualize where you want to go."

Toby put on the bracelet. The strap immediately constricted around his wrist, and he winced as he felt several pinpricks. Mr. Grimm confirmed they were biosensors injecting themselves into his skin.

A soft chime came from the craft's PA system and the unseen pilot alerted them that the penitentiary was just ahead and they had been cleared for landing. Lorna and Pete cupped their hands around the portholes. Through the rain-lashed glass, they could just see lights as they circled the island.

"Just for once I'd like to go somewhere that's hot," grumbled Lorna.

The tilt-rotor aircraft rotated, the twin engines gracefully angling into a vertical position so that it could descend onto the raised helicopter pad.

Inside the sound-dampened aircraft, nobody could hear the sudden warbling alarm echo across the island. Nor did they see the energy bolt rip out from ground level and destroy the starboard wing in a massive orange ball.

Toby ducked in shock as the wing next to him exploded in a massive fireball. Shrapnel smashed against the fuselage, shattering windows and tearing huge holes in the body—inches from Toby's head. The entire aircraft lurched ninety degrees to the side and dropped like a stone.

Cellblock H261 was an ultra-high-security wing designed for solitary confinement and built in the center of the island. Branching corridors radiated out in a starlike pattern from the central security hub, which was only approachable by an underground guard hut that boasted over twenty separate security checks.

Trojan bypassed it all as she stepped out of the wall and into the middle of the long sterile white corridor. Her huge cloak billowed impossibly large, revealing Basilisk and Worm walking out of the material as though they had simply strolled through a tunnel. Which, in a manner of speaking, they had.

Trojan had tried to explain that her supergift was nothing as primitive as teleportation but involved quantum tunneling; just as Worm burrowed through the ground from one point to another, she could burrow a short distance through space. Worm nodded in understanding, although her babbling was as clear to him as Basilisk trying to explain the Internet. How much simpler life was in the forties, he mused. People only had war to contend with.

Basilisk's cane clicked on the smooth metal floor as he led them down a corridor that had nothing other than a pair of security cameras in it. The architects had not thought anybody could get this far without triggering an alarm. At the end of the corridor was a lone door—Cell G. Basilisk knew that beyond the door there was a nullification field that would render their powers useless if they entered the cell, so even Trojan couldn't simply walk in and whisk their prize away, since she would be trapped too. They had to get through that door and retain their powers. He turned to Worm.

"Okay, your turn."

"Me? How can I get through that?"

Basilisk pointed to an electronic keypad at the side of the door. "Simple. Just worm your way into it."

Worm pressed his hands against the panel and allowed his fingertips to atomize and burrow into the pad's components. He closed his eyes, wincing at the pinprick sensations stabbing his fingers as he sensed every twist of wire or logical gate in the electronic processors. It seemed as though he was picking an old-fashioned combination lock blindfolded—except the combinations were digital. He didn't even have to try to calculate the complex codes, which could have taken months. He simply willed his probing atoms to pass through like water along an aqueduct. The lock bleeped, and after several seconds a loud clunk from within the fortified door signaled that the heavy mechanical bars had unlocked.

Breakout

With a hiss, the vacuum-sealed door swung back on hydraulic rams. The chamber was circular, lit only by a single recessed light. A solid steel block with a thin mattress formed a bed. No need for blankets, as the room was climate controlled. A young man sat on the edge of the bed, staring at the new arrivals.

"Greetings," said Basilisk.

"This is him?" Worm asked doubtfully.

Basilisk's voice oozed admiration. "You are looking at one of the most destructive forces on the planet. This is Viral."

Viral was no more than twenty-five, dressed in dirty black jeans and a crumpled black shirt. His long hair was ruffled, and his stubbly face was gaunt and pale with black-rimmed eyes. He looked like an ill Goth, which was an amazing achievement by anyone's standards. He regarded his saviors with a jaundiced eye.

"Who're you?"

"We're your ticket out of here. But you must do as I ask."

Viral considered for a moment as he gazed around his bare cell. "Not like I've got much going on here." He stood up and couldn't help but smile when his three rescuers quickly stepped backward. He gave Trojan an appraising look up and down as he shielded his eyes from the extra illumination in the corridor.

He grinned, showing yellow teeth. "What's the plan?"

Trojan shrugged. "I can get us out of here, but it's going to take a couple of minutes for me to recharge."

"Recharge?" Basilisk said impatiently. "You're a Prime!"

"Tunneling through walls or across open space is easy enough, but the more difficult the obstructions, the more it takes out of me. Takes a little while for me to get my energy reserves back. All teleportation powers are like that."

"We don't have a couple of minutes," intoned Worm, as the door at the far end of the corridor clunked open and a dozen armed Enforcers pushed through, having been alerted when they had finally looked at their security monitors. Seeing their prisoner escaping, they raised their heavy assault rifles.

"Open fire!"

Trojan gripped the hem of her cape and threw it in a wide arc—it expanded in size to almost the width of the corridor and then suddenly held rigidly in place. The bullets hit the solid cloak, some ricocheted off into the walls and ceiling. Sparks erupted at the feet of the Enforcers as some bullets bounced right back at them.

"Cease fire! Cease fire!" one of them yelled.

Trojan looked at her companions. "That's bought us several seconds. Now what?"

Breakout

Basilisk pushed past Trojan, her cloak dropping to the floor like a heavy sheet and retracting to its normal size as though made from elastic. The Enforcers were now faced with Basilisk, who was peeling his hood back.

"Open fire! Open fire!" yelled the same man who had just told them to stop. The Enforcers were confused by the conflicting orders—and that hesitation cost them dearly.

Basilisk's eyes gleamed. To the Enforcers, it was like looking into the sun, as they felt pain rack their bodies. The initial sudden jolt was replaced by a cool sensation like drifting in a frigid ocean. They were unaware that their bodies were being turned to stone from the outside in.

Only four of the Enforcers had the presence of mind to look away—but eight of their companions turned pale gray as their skin petrified. Within seconds they were nothing more than highly detailed stone statues.

The remaining Enforcers backed quickly through the door, and whoever was watching the security camera monitors had the presence of mind to hit the alarm.

Worm looked around as a siren warbled through the complex. "Not bad. Just another hundred or so more guards and we're scot-free."

"This escape plan sucks," sniffed Viral.

Basilisk ignored the jibe and advanced toward the hub. They would have to bide their time until Trojan could reenergize her powers. As he entered the hub he brushed past the petrified guards, who crumbled to dust. In the meantime he might as well have a little fun.

The hub was a massive hemispherical chamber with other high-security doors leading to a gallery of evil. In the middle of the room was an elevator column. The reinforced elevator doors swished closed, shielding the four fleeing guards. It was the only route out.

The other villains entered the room and Basilisk took several steps before he noticed that the security cameras in the room had swiveled round to face him. Seconds later, heavy-duty auto-guns lowered from the ceiling. Trojan threw up her cloak to protect the others, but Basilisk was beyond her reach and was forced to leap aside as the powerful sentry weapons tore up the floor around him.

The guns swiveled to track his progress, spent shell casings clattering to the floor. Several shots blew Basilisk's carbon-fiber cane apart and clipped his stone arms. Basilisk howled out in pain, but he didn't bleed. The bullets had merely cut grooves across his forearm. The hem of his cape suffered tennis-ball-sized holes. He responded by unleashing an energy blast from his fingers. An auto-gun exploded and fell, still suspended from the ceiling by thick cables and sparking electronics. The remaining two guns swiveled on him.

Breakout

He skillfully took them both out with an energy blast before they could take aim.

Trojan lowered her cloaking shield and Worm brushed dust from his robes.

"Impressive," said Worm.

Followed by Viral, they walked past Basilisk, who had his hand extended, expecting to be pulled to his feet. No assistance was forthcoming, so he painfully hauled himself upright and limped toward the elevator.

"Below this is another high-security chamber that will be heavily guarded. That will lead us outside into the compound." Basilisk spun to face Trojan. "By which time I expect you'll be ready to take us out of here."

Worm looked him up and down. "There will be plenty more guards waiting for us. You can't face many more. Look at the state you're in. And my talents do not lie in *direct* combat."

Basilisk met his gaze. That was something he had been wondering too. He had hoped Trojan would simply be able to transport them out, but as usual there were unforeseen problems. They could sit and wait, but that would mean giving the Enforcers more time to regroup and form a containment plan.

Viral spoke up, his voice no louder than a harsh whisper. "Leave them to me. I owe my captors for locking me away for so long."

* * *

The lower section of the hub was essentially the bottom part of the whole sphere. The walls curved inward to a wide floor space. The only exit was a sloping corridor that led to the inner-prison quadrangle, and yet more automated security.

The elevator came down in the center of the room, nothing more than a tube that lowered from the ceiling. Here there were no elevator doors to open; instead the tube simply rose up again to reveal the elevator's occupants like a kind of magic trick. This meant that, unlike the room above, there was no central column behind which an escaping felon could hide. The designers had called it "open-plan security."

Twenty Enforcers were crammed into the chamber in two tiers; the front row knelt to allow the row behind to fire. They all braced their weapons against their shoulders, took aim down the barrels of their state-of-the-art Heckler & Koch automatic weaponry, and rested their fingers on the triggers as the elevator descended from the ceiling.

Agonizing seconds passed before the elevator rose once more to reveal the elevator's lone occupant: Viral. He stood motionless in the middle of the chamber with his hands on his head. The sign of surrender made the Enforcers hesitate.

Breakout

The prisoner stood passively. The Enforcer commander felt he should say something.

"Um . . . don't move. Your little escape plan's over, pal."

What happened next was very quick. Viral nodded in understanding.

And then he sneezed.

For a few precious seconds the commander thought the prisoner was accepting his fate. Then one of the guards suddenly realized just who the prisoner was, but it was too late even to cover his mouth.

The sneeze shot out at a typical ninety-five miles per hour. It carried millions of airborne viruses that spread across the group of Enforcers in a little over three seconds. Viral had the power to create and spread a disease of his choosing, causing almost limitless effects.

Within five seconds every Enforcer in the room was lying on the ground clutching his stomach as sharp pains struck them. Their eyes bulged as their limbs stiffened in rapid rigor mortis. Within ten seconds every soldier was dead. Viral looked around at his handiwork with a thin smile. It had been years since he'd last exercised his power and it felt *great*.

The elevator lowered again and Basilisk, Worm, and Trojan appeared. They looked at the dead guards with a mix of admiration and apprehension.

"Amazing," said Trojan. "They weren't wrong about

you, were they? We're not gonna, like, catch something, are we?"

Viral winked at her. "My infection died the moment the guards did. You'll be fine."

Basilisk had trouble stepping over the Enforcers and winced every time he came into contact with one of the corpses. Worm retrieved a fallen gun, which looked comically huge against his diminutive size. He followed them out, using his sleeve to cover his mouth in case he inhaled the contaminant.

Basilisk dealt with the auto-guns in the corridor, but each energy blast was costing him his strength.

Outside, the alarms were louder than ever and Basilisk could see Enforcers running for cover. The sloping passage opened up in the middle courtyard. It was one hundred feet to the wall or any type of shelter. Again the open-plan security concept was working against him. He needed some form of protection.

Basilisk glanced up and saw a twin-engine aircraft come in to land. Its tilt-rotors moved from horizontal to vertical position as it hovered over a helipad on the roof of one of several facility buildings. That would provide just the protection they needed.

Gathering all his strength, Basilisk shot a mighty energy bolt from his hands, and then sagged to his knees. The bolt struck one of the engines, tearing off the wing. As he had anticipated, the aircraft rolled onto its side—and dropped onto the building below. Propelled by the remaining rotor the craft flipped off the building and came crashing into the courtyard as the second wing exploded—sending fragments of rotor in every direction. Enforcers positioned on the roof had to duck to avoid being decapitated.

Worm fired his stolen gun in random directions as they ran for the shelter offered by the downed aircraft. The recoil from the weapon almost knocked the little man off his feet. Once again, no help was offered to Basilisk, who had very little strength left in him. It took sheer willpower to force himself back on his feet and follow the others to the safety of the crashed aircraft.

Toby vowed never to travel in an airplane again. They just kept crashing. Dim red emergency lights were on, but smoke was filling the fuselage and he had to keep his head low so he could breathe. Any item that was not bolted down was now scattered across the floor . . . Toby corrected himself, scattered across the *ceiling*. The aircraft was upside down. He could feel the intense heat from the burning wings outside and it was only a matter of time before the interior caught fire.

"Lorna! Em? Pete?" he shouted. His eyes were beginning to sting now.

"We're here!" Emily shouted. The girls had bravely

dragged the unconscious pilot and copilot from the cockpit but there was no sign of Mr. Grimm. Emily had a cut across her cheek, but as Toby watched, it healed itself and vanished—a healing factor from her random powers. Lorna was next to her, with the neck of her jacket pulled up over her mouth to filter the smoke.

"Where's Pete?" he asked.

A tearing noise snatched their attention as a massive hole was torn in the side of the fuselage. Standing in the hole was a huge muscular figure that must be Pete—he had swollen biceps that made it look as though he had been pumping iron since birth. Toby himself had gone through a similar transformation when he faced Doc Tempest, but Pete's power was even more impressive as both arms were also aflame. And judging by Pete's lack of reaction, Toby correctly guessed the flames were another malfunctioning super-power that had crossed with the enhanced strength.

The courtyard was pandemonium. Pete hurled aside a chunk of fuselage that he had torn away to allow his friends to escape. The fuselage struck Worm and Viral, the force of the blow throwing them halfway across the yard. Basilisk watched in amazement as Pete strode from the wreckage.

"Supers!" he yelled in warning. Basilisk had assumed that the Primes would be running for cover, and with

Breakout

the Web site down, there would be no fake heroes like this bunch. They were yet another complication to his plan. Basilisk was starting to feel frustrated.

Enforcers gathered along the rim of the courtyard. They had no idea if the crashed plane was carrying heroes or more super-criminals for incarceration. They opted to play it safe and opened fire on everybody.

Toby, Emily, and Lorna ran from the blazing plane, dragging the pilots. They looked around in alarm as bullets chewed up the ground near their feet.

Lorna yelled at the top of her voice. "Stop shooting at us! We're on your side, you idiots!"

Emily instinctively raised a shield and an energy bubble encased them both—but it failed to stretch to Toby.

Toby leaped into the air without thinking and was relieved to discover that he could fly. He rose above the battle to get some idea of what was happening. He noticed Worm and Basilisk, the two main villains they had been briefed about. Basilisk seemed to have an injured leg, and was propped against the remains of the aircraft. Toby thought Worm's photographs did justice to just how ugly he was. His bright red cape made him an easy target and the brooch that clasped it together reflected the courtyard's searchlights. Its swirling design glinted in Toby's eyes.

Toby felt himself transfixed by the whirling motion. He could feel himself relax despite the chaos around him. In fact he couldn't think of any reason to do *any-thing* other than gaze at the shiny . . .

Pete moved into Toby's line of sight, breaking the spell. Toby shook his head to remove the hypnotic effect, and remembered Mr. Grimm's briefing had warned them about Worm's more archaic villain props such as the hypno-disk.

Toby noticed the other two villains. One he recognized from the briefing as Trojan and assumed the scrawny-looking Goth was Viral, the prisoner Grimm suspected they'd rescue.

Time to end this prison break, he thought.

Apart from the villains, the circle of Enforcers was the immediate threat to his friends. Toby noticed a portion of the aircraft's wing was angled against the courtyard wall; it would offer protection from the gunfire. He gestured to it as he yelled: "Lorna! Run for the wing! Get the pilots out of the line of fire!"

"Are you deaf? Stop shooting!" Emily screamed irritably, as the bullets continued striking. The Enforcers didn't listen, and she would have been surprised if such a simple plea convinced seasoned soldiers, anyway.

The intense flames that spread over Pete's body melted the bullets shot at him. He was only struck by molten metal, which felt, through his muscular body, like being hit by a paintball.

Breakout

Basilisk didn't have the strength for a three-way battle, and targeted the retreating girls.

Viral had picked himself up and fired a black mist at Pete. Pete retaliated with a whiplike strand of fire that incinerated the lethal virus swarm.

Toby was impressed with Pete's ability to adapt to the sudden change in situation. He tried to soar over Pete's assailant, but discovered he was fixed to the spot. Confused, he tried to gain altitude then lower himself, which he did without a problem—he just couldn't move *around*. With despair he recognized the power as something Pete had mistakenly downloaded when they took out some local gangsters a week ago—*levitation*.

Up and down was all he had.

Worm pulled himself from under the chunk of fuselage. He locked eyes with Toby—and for a brief second there was a vague glimmer of recognition, a connection . . . in the past? Impossible, of course. The sound of bullets pulled Worm back to the present. His powers were useless here, the solid rock under his feet meant he couldn't bury himself. Instead he decided the floating boy was an easy target as he hung above the battlefield, so turned his gun on him. The report from the gun made him close his eyes.

At the same time, a pair of Enforcers decided to take out the same target.

Toby cut the levitation power and dropped a few feet to the ground—just as multiple streams of bullets combed through the air where he had been moments before. He rolled to his feet and extended his hands in the hope he had some type of projectile power.

Luck was with him.

Worm opened his eyes to see if he had hit his target. The boy was now pointing at him—and a bolt of lightning flickered from his fingers and split Worm's gun in two.

Emily and Lorna tucked the pilots safely under the wing, but now Emily's shield started to waver—at first it rippled like jelly from the bullet impacts before it suddenly turned into water. The water-shield hung in the air for a split second, before splashing uselessly to the ground.

"Our powers are changing!" yelled Lorna as she dragged her friend to safety behind a burning fragment of aircraft wing.

Toby unleashed another lightning bolt. Electricity arced toward Worm—but then the lightning transformed into smoke.

Trojan had been keeping low behind her shield as the battle raged. Now she was feeling strong again. "Let's go!" she yelled as she whirled her cape around, expanding it.

Worm turned on his heels and sprinted away,

Breakout

galvanized when he saw Pete turn toward him—the flames now covered his body from head to foot.

Toby tore his gaze away from Pete, who was looking very impressive, and found Viral blocking his path. The villain gave a humorless grin and grabbed both of Toby's forearms before he could summon another power.

"They're sending kids in now to stop Viral? What an insult!"

Toby struggled, but the scrawny man was surprisingly strong. In fact, Toby was beginning to think his powers had abandoned him.

"Do you know what I can do?" growled Viral. "What exquisite agony I can cause?"

Toby met Viral's gaze and tried to hide his disgust at his yellow, bloodshot eyes. With a hiss, Viral's hands turned black and Toby's sleeves began to rot away as the material decayed. Toby felt a stab of pain as Viral's fingers dissolved the material and touched his wrists. He felt a burning sensation that made his knees tremble.

Summoning all his strength Toby pulled his arms away—and this time the superpowers surged back with such force that Viral howled as his arms were almost torn from their sockets. Toby turned and ran, not wishing to spend another second fighting the freak. Viral clawed and hooked Toby's jacket, trying to pull him back, but the material dissolved under his touch and fell off Toby—who fled.

The Enforcers stopped shooting, as they finally fig-ured out the bad guys from the good guys.

"Boy, come on! Time to go!" shouted Worm.

Worm's shout stopped Viral from pursuing Toby. More Enforcer bullets whizzed around him, causing him to retreat to the safe folds of Trojan's cape.

Basilisk hauled himself up and limped toward Trojan, but his leg gave way and he stumbled. He reached out—and suddenly felt a searing pain around his midriff as Pete wrapped both flaming hands around him and plucked him up like a toy. Basilisk's arms and legs flailed uselessly.

Basilisk watched with fury as Trojan wrapped her cape around Viral and Worm. She looked at him one last time with a hint of regret. Then her cape whirled to cover herself. Basilisk watched as it shrank into a point in space and vanished.

Basilisk howled in frustration. They had succeeded in freeing the one key component to their plan—but had abandoned their mastermind.

A New Perspective

Pete rubbed the sleep from his eyes. He was feeling exceptionally irritated at the latest turn of events and was releasing his anger at whoever dared speak to him.

When the villains vanished from Diablo Island, the Enforcers had ceased fire and started to yell to Pete to surrender Basilisk to them. Pete was still pumping fire from his body and standing a good six feet tall, holding Basilisk in a tight bear hug that miraculously didn't burn him to a crisp. But try as he might, Pete couldn't deactivate his powers and the more stressed he felt, the more spikes of fire leaped from his body in a threatening manner.

Toby looked nervously at Emily and Lorna. They all shared the same thought—it wasn't going to be long until the Enforcers fired again. Toby scanned the guards who circled them on the courtyard walls. Every rifle was slowly being raised. He took a split second to reach a decision.

"Let's get out of here!" Toby yelled as he yanked back

his sleeve and thumbed the teleport button on the wrist pad Mr. Grimm had given them.

The world flashed brilliantly and then they were standing in a field with the sun sinking on the horizon. Toby could see the lights of their hometown below, and when he turned to the others he blinked at the double unexpected surprise.

First, Basilisk lay unconscious on the ground, his cape still smoldering. Toby had automatically assumed the bracelet would teleport just them; he hadn't expected the supervillain to accompany them, even though Pete was holding him. The second surprise was to see Pete had still not returned to normal. It was a bizarre sight to watch a flaming giant fall to his knees, trying not to throw up from the dizzying effect of the teleportation. Even transformed, teleportation was an experience Pete just couldn't get used to.

Emily and Lorna could only watch as the flames flickered from Pete and lit the grass around him. Toby joined them in stamping out the fires that were popping up, and they shouted at him to calm down and try to kill his power.

It took a few minutes for Pete to relax. He tried to douse the flames by rolling in a rain puddle, but the liquid vaporized in a cloud of steam. It wasn't until he sat down and took a deep breath that the flames fizzled out and he shrank back to normal size.

A New Perspective

But that still left the unconscious supervillain. Pete and Toby used their belts to bind his hands together and hoped he wouldn't wake up anytime soon. Pete was about to pull the fiend's hood off—but Toby stopped him, reminding them all of Basilisk's petrification powers. Instead Pete tied his jacket over Basilisk's head as extra security.

It took all four of them to carry Basilisk, and the going was slow as they crossed the fields. Emily had tried to invoke some kind of superstrength, but it appeared that their powers were lying dormant for the time being.

The next problem was what to do with Basilisk. Pete and Toby both agreed that they could put him in Toby's garage, at least for a couple of hours, and gag him so that he wouldn't alert Toby's parents—but Lorna was adamantly against the idea. Toby was surprised at his sister's reaction and assumed the thought of having a supervillain in the house terrified her.

Emily's garage was in constant use. That left Pete, who pointed out that his family didn't even have a garage, let alone a car. Toby knew that they had a large shed, though, which Pete's parents never used. Pete had flat out refused—but eventually he gave in to his friends' constant pressure, even though he felt it was borderline bullying.

An hour later, Pete found himself in his dark shed

with nothing but a flashlight. Basilisk was still unconscious, now with a sack over his head, and a gag around
that. He was bound with a thick electrical extension
cable they had used instead of rope. Pete was angry that
his friends had predictably all made excuses to return
home, leaving him alone to guard the prisoner.

He sat, stewing in his own misery and rage. From
here he could hear shouting coming from the open
kitchen window of his house. Yet again his parents
were fighting. It had become a regular thing, and he
was finding it harder and harder to ignore. Even though
they stopped shouting if he was in the room, he could
feel the bitter tension between them. He decided that
being cooped up in a shed with a captive supervillain
was better than facing the wrath of his parents.

Toby was going to lend Pete his cell phone, but discovered that he had lost it in the tussle with Viral.
Lorna volunteered her phone in case Pete needed any
help. Now he stared at the screen, wondering if he
should call Toby to chat about *something* to relieve the
boredom, but decided against it. If anything, finding
Hero.com had weakened their bond of friendship.

Access to Hero.com was a constant sticking point. Pete
was also starting to resent Toby's automatic assumption
that he was team leader. When Pete had suggested creating a team name and a set of superhero costumes, Toby
had been the first to shoot the idea down. The more he

thought about it, the more obvious it became that Hero.com was not a gift—it was a curse, ruining friendships and placing them constantly in danger.

But it was also an escape route out of his problems at home and at school. Pete speculated how much more fun it would have been if he'd found the Web site alone. It would have been his secret and he could have used those powers to help himself out of the miserable life he currently had.

He thought of calling Emily, but lately he had found himself becoming nervous when talking to her. He hoped he wasn't developing a crush—that would be *awful*. But then again, she seemed to be interested in Toby.

Typical—his friend was taking *everything* from him.

That left nobody else he could call. The hollow feeling that had been growing inside his stomach seemed that much bigger.

Basilisk stirred and immediately struggled against his bonds, his angry cursing muffled by the gag.

"Take it easy," said Pete, trying to keep the tremor of fear from his voice. "You're being held captive by . . . by . . ."

He was stuck for a superhero name. Because none of them possessed specific powers, it was difficult to brand themselves. But *"Pete"* was hardly threatening.

"We're working for the Hero Foundation so don't

try anything. Unless you want me to smother you in flames again."

Basilisk calmed down and mumbled something incoherent. Pete hesitated. He had promised the others he wouldn't remove the sack or the gag, but right now he had nobody to talk to. He might as well interrogate the prisoner.

"I'm going to remove your gag. Scream out and you'll get a, uh, lightning bolt to the head. Understand?"

"Urgh-uh," Basilisk replied.

Pete took that for a yes and tentatively walked around Basilisk and untied the gag, though he made sure to keep the sack firmly over Basilisk's face. The villain took a deep breath.

"You're a Downloader?"

"Yes. And a lot of very angry people want to talk to you about putting the virus into our system." He moved a large, dingy, cracked bathroom mirror from a stool and sat down.

"The virus was a mere taste of things to come," said Basilisk levelly. "Nothing compared to the imminent downfall of your precious little Foundation. Then you will once again be nothing more than an ordinary child."

The words stung Pete, especially the word *ordinary*.

Basilisk continued. "In fact I'm surprised you're still able to download powers."

"We were the only ones who could. But they're a

A New Perspective

little glitchy." The words were out of his mouth before he realized he'd given almost everything away.

"Most interesting. Just you four left, eh?"

"There are others," retorted Pete sharply.

Basilisk knew he had the upper hand despite the circumstances. He poured on the scorn. "You mean the Primes? The *real* heroes, not toy heroes like you and your friends. Well, I didn't see the Primes flying around Diablo Island. And I don't hear them rushing to your aid now."

Pete nervously checked the knots that held Basilisk in place and hoped they were strong enough. No matter how much superstrength Basilisk possessed he did not have the leverage to snap the wire, at least that's what Lorna had explained. Pete was beginning to have doubts about that and he fingered the mobile in his pocket.

"Most Primes are nothing but cowards; well, the so-called heroic ones. Not like me and my oppressed brethren. We put our necks on the line whereas the people you work for hide behind children like you."

Pete hated to admit it, but he agreed with the villain's viewpoint. Their mission to Diablo Island had just confirmed that.

"So destroying the competition is what you had in mind?" asked Pete.

"An interesting way of putting it. Maybe you're not

as simpleminded as your friends . . . " Basilisk paused for a long moment, his head moving around as though he could clearly see around the shed, "who are not here. I take it then that you must be their leader. The brave one to interrogate the archvillain before handing him in?" He paused for effect. "I assume that to be the truth as no hero would leave their friend alone with a notorious criminal such as I. Would they?"

Pete remained silent for fear of openly agreeing with him. He thought about his friends sitting in their comfortable homes, and bet that they didn't have their parents arguing in the background.

He had never felt so lonely.

Toby thumped the mouse hard; the Web site was still off-line. He had tried to search for "VIRAL" as a supervillain, but the regular Internet turned up nothing useful. He needed the rogues' gallery on Hero.com to find more information about who they had faced. Plus, he needed to tell the authorities that they had captured Basilisk, but the site's e-mail was down and there had been no sign of Mr. Grimm. Toby was beginning to think he must have died in the crash.

Toby stifled a yawn and felt incredibly tired—it had been a long day after all. He knew he should call Pete to make sure things were okay with Basilisk. Then

A New Perspective

again, Pete hadn't called him, so he took that as a sign all was well.

His thoughts were interrupted as his e-mail pinged. Toby saw the message was from UNKNOWN. He hesitated; it looked like spam—unwanted e-mails sent to thousands of in-boxes, either coaxing people's bank details from them or containing viruses. Usually he deleted such messages as soon as they arrived. His finger hovered over the delete key, but again he hesitated. It could be somebody trying to get in touch with him. He clicked on the e-mail.

A message flashed across the screen. "VIDEO FEED ACTIVATED." Toby blinked in surprise. He glanced at the Webcam sitting on top of the monitor and quickly tried to flatten his hair, which was wild after his shower. A video window opened on-screen and Chameleon's serious face appeared. Toby's elation at seeing the superhero was quickly flattened when he realized he was dressed in very unheroic pajamas.

"Toby, good to see you in one piece," said Chameleon with a curt nod. "I must be brief, there is much happening. First of all, congratulations. Not many face Viral and live to tell the tale."

Toby unconsciously rubbed his wrist, just under the wristband they all still wore. The encounter with Viral had left two black marks where the villain's fingers had touched. They didn't feel like bruises and no amount of scrubbing would get rid of them. "So you know about what happened? That we have Basilisk?"

"Yes. That is why I had to contact you. Basilisk is a lethal customer. Do you have him in a secure facility?"

Toby hesitated. He wasn't so sure a garden shed counted as secure. "He's with Pete. Locked up tight."

"Good. It is imperative you let nobody see him, and don't talk to him; he can be silver-tongued when it suits him. Mr. Grimm will be on his way with a retrieval force, but it won't be until daylight."

"Grimm's alive? I thought he'd abandoned us. And why not until tomorrow?"

"Mr. Grimm is not a fighter, so he had no part to play. That was *your* duty." He was a typical Prime then, a coward at heart, not a hero. "And because things are so chaotic we cannot rally enough forces to retrieve him any sooner. The disaster on Diablo Island means more Enforcers are needed to try and secure the rest of the prison. We have a riot situation there now. The Hero Foundation is stretched thin. And while you may have captured Basilisk, Worm and Trojan escaped with Viral."

Toby thought he detected a note of blame in Chameleon's voice. "We were unprepared for Diablo Island, and your guards there didn't exactly help the situation by shooting at us. So what's so special about this team anyway?"

A New Perspective

"Trojan is able to infiltrate very secure areas with ease. Worm can now enter computer systems and override them. And Viral's skills are not just confined to the physical world—he has the ability to create digital viruses that cannot be stopped. The three of them together are a recipe for disaster. With Hero.com off-line it is probable they will try to locate our headquarters, infiltrate our physical defenses, and topple the Foundation . . . leaving them access to our stored superpowers."

The reality hit Toby. "That's terrible!"

"It gets worse. They could twist Hero.com, transforming it into a private Villain.net, under their control."

Toby didn't know what to say. It was because of his team's failure that these villains were still loose.

Chameleon continued. "That is why, once we have Basilisk safely in custody, your team will have to locate Worm and the others."

"They could be anywhere in the world!"

"Your primary mission is to defend the Foundation. The Enforcers, and a few Primes not in hiding, are trying to protect the public from increasingly hostile villainous activity. The rest of it is up to you. Find Worm and the others and stop their plan. Worm will have a hideout somewhere. You just have to locate it."

"Do you have any leads?"

"I'm afraid not. Commander Courage, the hero who runs the Foundation, was the one who fought Worm in the past and imprisoned him—but something truly awful happened to Courage shortly afterward and he fell into a coma, suffering severe amnesia for a number of years. When he finally woke, he had no recollection of what had happened or *where* he'd imprisoned Worm."

"How is that possible?"

"There are many terrible things in this world we still don't fully understand. And Courage was a victim of that." Chameleon stared straight at the camera. "I know this is a great burden, but whether you feel ready or not, *you're* our only hope out there."

Toby awoke the next morning still feeling exhausted. His conversation with Chameleon had not lifted his spirits.

Toby's mother was shouting at him to get dressed and his eyes shot to the clock: 9:00 a.m. He bolted from bed at an incredible speed. In a split second he was standing at his bedroom door fully dressed as his blankets were still falling from the bed—that assured him he still had superpowers. Then he realized that he wasn't late for school—it was the scheduled day off.

He should have phoned Pete last night but instead had gone straight to bed and fallen asleep the moment his head hit the pillow.

Toby shouted to his mother that he was awake and

getting dressed, then picked up the phone and dialed Lorna's cell number. Several seconds passed before Pete picked it up, and spoke with a groggy voice.

"Yeah?"

"Pete, it's Tobe. How're you? Everything okay?"

"Uh . . . I . . . I was asleep."

"Is Basilisk safe?"

Toby heard a loud yawn before Pete answered with a flat, unenthusiastic voice. Not the usual Pete. "He's still in my shed if that's what you mean."

"Look, man, I'm sorry I didn't call last night. I fell asleep. But I talked to Chameleon. They're coming to pick Basilisk up today. I'll come over."

"Today? Uh . . . "

Toby frowned. "What's wrong?"

There was an unusually long silence broken by a loud snuffling as if Pete had just blown his nose. "My . . . uh . . . my parents. They said they're splitting up. I don't know what to do. Don't tell anyone, okay?"

Toby froze. Pete's parents constantly argued—it was the usual background noise to life in the Kendall household. But this was a bombshell, and Toby knew Pete would not take it well. Coupled with the fact that a supervillain was held prisoner in his shed and a platoon of Enforcers were coming to retrieve him—well, that was not going to help the situation.

"Okay, I'm coming over. See you in half an hour."

He ran downstairs at a more normal speed and started putting on his sneakers. He looked up to see his mother and father staring at him. They seemed over-dressed in business suits.

"Where do you think you're going?" Sarah Wilkinson asked firmly.

"Pete's. He needs me to—"

"No you're not. Today is the first day of your father's exhibition, remember?"

Toby rolled his eyes. "Aw, no!"

John Wilkinson wagged his finger. "We never ask you for much. You can at least come along for my first day and show some support."

Sarah nodded. "And since you're conveniently out of school, you're going to be there."

Toby had completely forgotten the public opening. "Oh, Mom! It's a day off!"

"You don't get something for nothing," warned his dad. "You've got tomorrow all to yourself."

"I really can't. I have to see Pete."

"You can see him in the afternoon," snapped Sarah in a voice that indicated the discussion was over. "But right now you can support your father! Lorna has already flitted out this morning leaving a note saying she's on a date. A *date*! And so early in the morning! I'll be having words with her tonight. She is going to be grounded for being so inconsiderate!"

A New Perspective

Toby was furious. He wished that he could snap back with the fact that *he* had saved her from the deadly clutches of Doc Tempest in Antarctica, and how *he* had saved his father's life by ensuring his plane could land. But of course they wouldn't believe him. He sighed deeply—just when his friend really needed him, he couldn't be there. He knew Pete would be mad at him—no, scratch that, *furious*—but he had asked Toby not to tell anyone. Toby couldn't face an argument over the phone. He decided to text Pete instead—but it wasn't until he was on his way with his parents in the car that he remembered he'd lost his cell phone.

Worm looked across the jungle canopy and listened to the chorus of insects that called it home. He heard footsteps on the stone floor and saw, from the corner of his eye, that Trojan had joined him. The humidity had caused her to pull her hood off, and her fine bobbed blonde hair fell to her shoulders as she examined Toby's cell phone.

"This fell out of the kid-hero's jacket pocket."

Worm glanced at it and frowned. "What on earth is it?"

Trojan sighed. Worm was still learning about the twenty-first century. "It's a cell phone . . . a telephone," she corrected herself.

"A telephone? But what about the wires? The exchange?"

"It's wireless," she sighed. "It uses . . . it's magic, okay?"

Worm snatched it from her. "How intriguing." He twisted it in his hands, almost snapping the clamshell screen off. "But so what? I have wireless communication equipment here at my base."

"What? A pigeon? The stuff you have here is ancient! And none of us know Morse code. We can't do *anything* with your stuff. Look, with this phone we can track the kid down. Find out where they've taken Basilisk."

Worm handed back the phone, then turned his gaze back across the jungle in thoughtful silence.

Trojan folded her arms and stared at the back of his head. "I mean, that's the plan. Right? He is the leader of this operation. Not you."

Worm whirled around, his blunt face red with anger. Trojan momentarily thought that his face almost did resemble a worm, albeit a worm with beady eyes and a thin mouth. "He is my *prisoner*! I should never have listened to his nonsense. And now I'm left babysitting you and Viral!"

Trojan gave him a crooked smile. She controlled her anger amazingly well for a villain. Then again, she preferred cunning theft rather than blatant action.

"Chill out before you give yourself a heart attack, Gramps."

A New Perspective

"I'd 'chilled out' long enough in this damn suspended animation chamber."

He kicked a central steel cylinder that dominated the ancient stone room. It was surrounded by control desks sporting huge dials and valves. State-of-the-art equipment for the 1940s, but now it looked like something out of an old black-and-white horror film.

Trojan shrugged. "You don't appreciate just how ingenious Stone Head's plan is."

"You know the full plan?"

"Not every detail. But with the three of us together and his knowledge of the enemy, it's a no-brainer. The Hero Foundation and the Council of Evil are the biggest threats we face in our profession. Paperwork is what's killing us now, not secret weapons or special powers. By assembling Viral and me, and even a geriatric like you, Basilisk has put into motion events that can really change the shape of history."

Spittle shot from Worm's mouth. "Geriatric! How dare you?" He stepped threateningly toward Trojan, but she just laughed at him. Being taller, she stopped his advance by pushing against his head.

"When Stone Head's plan brings down the cowering heroes we can form our own rival Council, helped by freeing those unfortunates held in Diablo Island. The real greats of our time like Lord Eon!" She blinked at Worm's lack of reaction. "Of course, he was after your time. The only Prime who can manipulate time! I always thought he was cool. Think what we could do if we freed *him*. Under our guidance, of course."

Worm calmed down; it was not wise to show any weakness in front of this calculating woman. Anger was a weakness; that was what had got him captured so many years ago.

"So, Old Timer, if you're tired of babysitting, and Stone Head neglected to reveal the intricate details of his plan to you . . . I don't think we have much of a choice than to go and save him. Do we?"

Worm nodded. "How do you propose we locate him with a mere telephone?"

"You'd make a lousy detective. The boy has a few friends in the address book stored in his phone. We can track their phone signal down and that will lead us to the boy and Basilisk. We should start with the last number dialed. Some girl named Lorna."

"You can track a cell phone signal?" asked Worm incredulously. He was bewildered by how much information was available through technology.

Trojan raised a perfect eyebrow. "Police do it all the time. It will lead us *right* to our target."

It was stiflingly warm inside the museum and it was packed, adding to the claustrophobic atmosphere.

A New Perspective

Normally Toby enjoyed walking around the exhibits, examining nasty-looking Viking or Indian weapons, marveling at the cool hieroglyphic texts of the ancient Egyptians, or staring at the dinosaur skeletons and imagining the beasts stamping around the countryside.

Unfortunately, today he was confined to the special exhibit hall that was showcasing his father's latest discovery. It was all very impressive the first time around—but the hundredth time around of hearing *exactly* the same story was tiring Toby. Plus a museum wasn't the place to be when you knew the fate of the free world hung on your shoulders. But how do you explain that to your parents?

He gazed at the photographs of the huge stepped pyramid that his father had discovered, hidden by foliage deep in the Mexican jungle. Its sides reached over the tree line, but were covered in so much vegetation that they blended into the jungle like a hill. It was just part of a lost city his father's expedition had uncovered, so new that it still hadn't been given a name. The surprising thing was that such a structure had remained hidden in this day and age. But then again, Toby knew that marvels could still be found in the world.

Toby stood at his father's side. His dad was giving an enthusiastic summary of the exhibition to a small knot of fascinated visitors. His zeal hadn't waned in the last

three hours. Toby had even caught his mom hiding a yawn on more than one occasion.

"We only made it into the outer chamber. The secrets of the inner chamber still remain for our next expedition. You can see from the aerial photographs that it resembles the site at Chichén Itzá, except here we have two symmetrical pyramids that . . . "

Toby zoned out. He had always liked the stories of the ancient Mayans, especially their version of basketball called *Pok-ta-pok*, which was played with a small rubber ball that the players had to keep off the ground using any parts of their body, except their hands. They had to get it through tiny sideways stone hoops on a wall. And sometimes the losers were killed. Gruesome, but great.

Toby sighed and glanced at his watch. Only two more hours to go. He hoped that Pete was okay and that the Enforcers had already taken Basilisk from him. He felt sorry for Pete and wished that he'd paid more attention to the fact his friend had not been himself the last few weeks. Then there was the problem of tracking Worm down. Chameleon had given him no help at all on that. He glanced at his watch again to double-check the time . . . then his eye was drawn to something on an exhibition photograph.

Something familiar.

Frowning, Toby squeezed between a couple of artsy

types to get a better view. It was an enlarged still of the pyramid's door. Toby had seen it dozens of times on his dad's jerky video diary. But here it was much clearer, a familiar swirling logo that had been incorrectly identified as a snake.

It was the *same* logo as the one on Worm's brooch, the one that had momentarily hypnotized Toby on Diablo Island. Mr. Grimm had warned them about Worm's old-school techniques, but Toby and Lorna had not paid any attention to such a small detail.

A horrible realization dawned on Toby. It was his own father who had discovered Worm's resting place; his own father who had unwittingly unleashed the supervillain, leading to events that would ultimately topple the Hero Foundation and destroy the world.

Toby felt sick.

Now more than ever he needed to talk to Pete. He just hoped there was not going to be any more bad news.

Pete sat in his dark bedroom and stared at the posters on his wall; some of them were fading with age. He had cried most of the night, but then had abruptly stopped as the sadness he had been feeling was replaced by numbness. He slipped Lorna's phone into his pocket since it was clear that Toby was not going to show up or even bother calling. After a two-hour wait, he finally realized his friends were about as reliable as his parents.

The only good news of the day was that his parents had left the house that morning. His mother was going to see friends and his dad was going to a bar, so it was quiet for a change and he wouldn't have to explain the arrival of the Enforcers to them. Whenever *they* bothered showing up.

Pete went into the kitchen for a glass of water. He slipped a straw in and went out to the shed, hoping that his prisoner hadn't died of thirst.

Basilisk's head shot up when Pete entered. Pete put the straw under the rim of the sack and Basilisk emptied the glass in one gulp.

"I heard shouting last night. I was worried you had been hurt," said Basilisk in a concerned tone.

"It's none of your business," snarled Pete. "And why would you be worried about me?"

"Because if you died, then maybe I would die alone in this cell?" Pete glanced around the flimsy wooden shed. "Your friends never came to interrogate me. So I presume without you, I would be alone in this place."

"Huh," said Pete. One person had bothered to call last night, Emily. But when Pete had seen her name on his caller ID he'd hesitated too long before answering and she hung up. As lonely as he was, he'd felt too miserable to speak to anyone.

A New Perspective

"So how did you become leader of such an irreverent group of heroes?"

"I'm not their leader," Pete snapped back, again silently cursing himself that he'd said too much.

"Surely somebody as talented and brave as you would be an inspiring leader, not a follower?"

At some level, Pete knew that Basilisk was just trying to butter him up. But right now the one thing he needed was positive encouragement.

"I agree with you. But I wouldn't let it worry you too much because the Enforcers are on their way as we speak. You're going to have a nice long time to think about it in Diablo Island. And when Hero.com is back online I will be the one making a difference and calling the shots."

Basilisk's voice echoed his concern. "Enforcers? Coming here?"

"When they bother showing up," said Pete, looking out of the dirty window.

"Did you know there's another way to get powers other than that juvenile Web site of yours?"

"Yeah, I know. Villain.net. I heard about that. But it's not as good as our site, rip-offs never are. You just end up with a poor quality copy," Pete mocked.

The ground suddenly started to shake. Jars of screws and nails scattered across the shelves and smashed on the floor. Pete gripped the door frame for support, convinced it was an earthquake.

"A pity you think so. I was hoping to find a more amicable solution rather than just killing you."

Pete whirled around to see a fine laser extend from Basilisk's finger and vaporize the electrical cable that was binding him. He stood up, kicking the chair away and tearing the sack from his head. His face was still obscured by his hood.

"You could escape? Then why did you wait?"

"I was waiting for *my friends* to turn up," mocked Basilisk. "You see, I have some. And here they are."

The muddy grass that Pete called a lawn suddenly erupted in a shower of dirt as the *Nematode* leaped from the ground and smashed through the neighbors' fence as the machine thudded to the ground like a soaring whale.

The vibrations from the *Nematode* were so intense that the flimsy shed shook itself apart. Pete shielded his head as the rotted roof crashed around him.

"No!" he bellowed and extended his hands to hurl a fireball or energy blast at Basilisk. Nothing happened. Pete panicked and willed himself aflame—still nothing.

The hatch of the *Nematode* flipped down, revealing a staircase, like in old-fashioned airplanes. Trojan jumped out, Viral following down the steps at a more leisurely pace.

"Seems you are all washed up, little man," Basilisk said with a laugh. "Now let me look at you!"

A New Perspective

Basilisk's eyes flared blue. To Pete the light seemed to fill his vision. He felt his chest constrict and he raised his hand protectively—the tips of his fingers turned cool. He suddenly recalled Mr. Grimm's briefing on the villain's powers—the petrification gaze. Pete worked on impulse and remembered a computer game he'd played. It was based on an ancient Greek legend of Perseus battling Medusa, whose gaze would turn any-body to stone. He grabbed a broken bathroom mirror that was poking from the shed rubble and turned it on Basilisk.

Basilisk suddenly howled as he stared at his own reflection. He tore his gaze away as the tip of his hood started to petrify. Pete dropped the mirror and scrambled backward into the yard, slipping on the mud and dropping to all fours.

He felt a hand grip his shoulder and yank him around. Mud splashed across his glasses and it was a moment before he could see the pale face of Viral staring at him.

"You're not going anywhere, squirt."

Pete gritted his teeth and lashed out, hoping to push the slimeball away. The wristband Grimm had given him hit Viral. The impact must have triggered something because a blast of energy erupted from his fingers and hurled Viral several feet until he slammed into the *Nematode* with a dull clang. Pete stood up, waves of energy crackling across his clenched fists.

Basilisk limped up the machine's staircase and spared a quick glance at Pete. "Kill him!"

The commotion had alerted Pete's neighbors, who came out to complain about the huge bronze machine that had appeared in their yards.

"What's going on here?" said a potbellied man wearing a thick sweater and unfashionably bright pants.

"Mr. Richards! Run!" screamed Pete.

The man opened his mouth to reply but Trojan turned on him and waved her arms as though throwing a Frisbee. She shot discus-shaped plasma at the man and blew him backward through his greenhouse window.

Pete fired an energy bolt at Trojan. It went wide and took out his kitchen window. Trojan whipped around and tossed another discus in retaliation. It hit Pete square in the chest—catapulting him through several neighboring fences in quick succession before he splashed into the pond of a house six doors down.

"Let me finish the runt off!" snarled Viral as he stalked toward Pete.

More neighbors were peering from their homes as Viral walked across perfectly manicured lawns, the grass turning black and decayed under his feet. One man emerged from his house wielding a baseball bat and clobbered Viral over the back of the head. The Goth went down.

"Teach you to trespass!" the man roared.

A New Perspective

Viral rubbed his head and gave the man a wicked grin.

The baseball bat turned black in the man's hands as the wood quickly rotted away. He dropped the blackened stump, and when he looked up, Viral was standing right in front of him. He snapped a hand around the man's throat. Immediately his flesh began to turn black and the man gagged for air.

A fireball whacked into Viral, breaking his deadly grip, leaving the man curled up on the ground, but alive. Viral was blown back through a standing portion of fence and rolled out the flames on the damp grass.

"I guess you're not fireproof, disease-boy," growled Pete, his own hands aflame. The neighbors who were still brave enough to be watching gasped in astonishment as their quiet young neighbor charged forward with a battle cry.

Basilisk watched the events from the *Nematode*'s doorway. "What are you waiting for? It's only one superbrat. Eliminate him!"

A deep thumping noise caught his attention and he looked up to see three twin-rotor Chinook helicopters roar low over the houses. They were black, with the Enforcers' insignia on the rear and weapon pods strapped to the sides of the machine.

"You're all under arrest!"

Basilisk leaned into the *Nematode* and shouted to

Worm, who was still seated at the controls. "Do you have anything in this piece of junk to bring those helicopters down?"

Worm was staring at the flying machine in fascination. "I have a sonic cannon. It was able enough against Spitfires during the war. I remember—"

Basilisk cut him off. "Use it!"

Viral stood up and wiped the blood from his nose. He stared at it in surprise. "I'm bleeding!"

Pete was in no mood to listen. He slung another fireball at the villain. Viral ducked and the blast ripped into a patio of the house behind him; the intense heat melted the double-glazing and set fire to several well-tended plants and Christmas decorations inside.

Viral didn't hang around. He sprinted toward the *Nematode*. Pete raced in pursuit, only stopping when he noticed the sonic cannon rise from the top of the ship. The weapon looked like a stretched bullhorn. It pivoted on a clockwork assembly toward one of the Chinooks. Then a bass-heavy roar blasted from the device. Pete felt his ribs vibrate and his teeth chatter as the sound wave rolled out and hit the aircraft.

The helicopter tried to bank away, but the sound blast sheared the front rotor and shattered the cockpit windows. The craft lurched down, out of control.

Pete watched in horror as the Chinook roared overhead and plowed into a house two doors down from where he lived. The helicopter tore straight through the roof in a shower of slates and crashed into the street on the other side of the building.

The remaining two helicopters responded by firing missiles from their weapon pods. Pete watched as one missile struck the side of the *Nematode*. The machine lurched, throwing Basilisk clear. The second missile blew Pete's patio to smithereens. The final two were wide of their mark and hit the upper floor of his house. Pete watched in dismay as a huge hole punched through the masonry, destroying his bathroom.

Trojan threw up her cape to shield herself from falling bricks. With her other hand she hurled a plasma disk at the Enforcers. The disk scraped the under-carriage of the chopper as it thundered overhead, but otherwise left it unharmed.

The *Nematode* moved on its bristling spikes and righted itself. Viral and Trojan ran for the stairwell.

Pete snarled under his breath. "You're not getting away with this!"

He sprinted forward. The sonic cannon spun around to track another Chinook.

Inside the *Nematode*, Worm was having the time of his life. It had been more than sixty years since he'd had a chance to play with his gadgets, and he was chuckling happily.

By the time Pete had reached the steps of Worm's

machine, the sonic cannon had fired again. Being this close to the cannon made his head feel as if it would rip in two.

The targeted helicopter orbited the battle zone, but Worm had had experience fighting the faster Spitfires during World War II. The blast hit the Chinook along the central fuselage and tore the helicopter in two—both halves sporting their own rotors.

Pete couldn't pull his gaze away as he saw Enforcers flung from the two halves of the chopper. The fuselages rotated wildly around, counter to the rotors. The lead half of the chopper zipped over the *Nematode*, forcing Pete to throw himself flat on the ground as the rotors swished narrowly overhead and sliced a groove across the machine's bronze bodywork, before smashing into Pete's living room with the force of a wrecking ball. The second portion of the Chinook followed and took out the roof of a neighbor's house as it fell into the street beyond.

Pete lifted himself up, covered in mud and fueled by anger. He jumped up the *Nematode*'s boarding steps and almost ran into Trojan as she poked her head out. She looked at him in surprise as he brought his arms around to fire at her point-blank.

But he never made it. A solid stone fist clunked him on the back of the head, knocking him unconscious.

The remaining Enforcer Chinook circled around,

A New Perspective

trying to get a decent shot, but the smoke pouring from the row of damaged houses obscured the scene below. Switching to thermal cameras, they watched as Basilisk dragged Pete's body into the *Nematode*. Seconds later the antique craft rumbled forward, digging through more gardens as it chewed into the ground.

The Chinook fired a salvo at the machine, but the rockets only managed to blow apart a few yard gnomes. The supervillains were gone—leaving a swathe of destruction and taking Pete with them.

01101000010010101110010010011

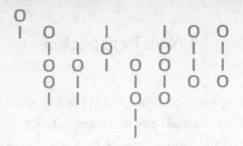

Welcome to the Jungle

The soda can was crushed to a ball of tin the size of a marble under Toby's extra-strong grip. He threw the metal into the corner of the SUV and glared at Mr. Grimm, who was sitting opposite him in his pristine black suit. The only mark he seemed to have after the plane crash on Diablo Island was what looked like a bite on his forehead.

Toby had regretted leaving Pete alone with Basilisk, and now he didn't even know if his friend was still alive. He was feeling guilty. He had taken the role of leader, but had done little to be proud of. He'd had enough and had shouted at Grimm that his friend was missing. Initially, Grimm had only been concerned with the mass hypnotism they'd have to perform so the residents of Pete's neighborhood would forget the day's events. The damage would have to be covered with a story of an exploding gas pipe or a plane crash. Toby, Lorna, and Emily listened in silence as Grimm lamented that the Prime they needed to make people really forget was a guy called Psych. He didn't hypnotize, he *rewired* people's brains. It was a shame he was in hiding.

"Are you sure about this?" Mr. Grimm asked after Toby had calmed down and explained how he'd matched the symbol on his father's discovery with the one on Worm's brooch. It was a tenuous link to Worm's lair, but Mr. Grimm had agreed it was the right place to start looking.

"It's the only lead we have," said Toby. "And we all owe it to Pete to save him."

Toby glanced at Lorna and Emily who sat in guilty silence. Lorna had been grounded after she had returned from her mystery date. When Toby had explained what he had found at Pete's house, or rather the remains of it, she instantly agreed to help. She had to sneak out and there would be trouble when she got home, but she couldn't worry about that right now.

"Since your flying powers are haphazard at best, the Foundation has an aircraft waiting for you," said Mr. Grimm. "It will take you through Mexican airspace, under radar so you don't get shot down. After that, I'm afraid you are on your own."

Toby stared at him. "Not that you've been much of a help to begin with."

Mr. Grimm stared unblinkingly at him. "We are over-stretched, as I have explained to you at every possible occasion."

"While you all have been hiding and throwing us to the supervillains out there, we've been risking our lives to prevent this gang from destroying the Hero Foundation." Mr. Grimm straightened his already perfect tie and Toby assumed he'd hit a nerve.

"Like true heroes. Selfless sacrifice." Toby was sure he saw the flicker of an ironic smile when Grimm said that. He didn't entirely trust the man. "Remember, heroes are not made by powers or abilities. They are made by action and attitude. And I did not abandon you. I teleported out as soon as the plane went down, as I thought you would too."

"I thought being a hero is a state of mind? Well, thanks to you, Pete may be dead and Basilisk is back on the loose."

Mr. Grimm refused to meet Toby's accusing gaze and instead studied a computer monitor. A blip flashed over the northeast arm of Mexico. "We have a position for him. We're still picking up a faint signal from Lorna's cell."

"I hope he doesn't make any calls," said Lorna. It was the first thing she had said since they had been picked up by Mr. Grimm. "Mom would kill me if I got another huge phone bill."

Mr. Grimm shook his head. "It's switched off."

Emily looked up. "Off? How can you trace a phone if it's off?"

Welcome to the Jungle

"You can remotely activate a phone, its microphone, or even its camera without the end user ever knowing. Although there seems to be some sort of interference stopping us from doing that. The FBI call it a Roving Bug; the only way to stop it is by removing the battery." He typed a few commands on the keyboard. "He has been stationary since we began tracing. Perhaps he is in a prison?"

"Or dead," Emily said in a low voice. She was the only one who had tried to call Pete. She should have known something was wrong when he didn't answer. Tears rolled from her eyes and she fought not to cry out loud.

"A possibility," said Grimm in his irritatingly calm voice. "But you must remember, above everything else, that this is a chance to stop Basilisk's plan. His actions have upset the balance between good and evil around the globe. And a stable balance is something the world needs in order to function. As we speak, world governments are fighting villains who are capitalizing on the situation. Everywhere, crime is on the rise and unless we stop Basilisk and his gang, things will only get worse. We need to create more heroes to bring back the status quo."

They understood the gravity of his words, but from where they were sitting in the back of the vehicle the rest of the world seemed to be functioning as usual.

"Don't you mean we need more heroes to *win*?" asked Toby.

"Win? Well, that would be terrible!"

The three friends exchanged glances.

"But I thought that was the point," said Emily.

"A world run by superheroes would bring about more trouble than you could imagine. If everybody thought they were right, then soon divisions would appear, and divisions cause conflict. Conflict causes war."

Toby was thinking hard. "But it would be two hero sides fighting . . . would that be so bad?"

"It would be *two forces* fighting. Both would think the other a villain. No, a balance is always needed. What good is light without shade to hide in?"

Toby's mind reeled at the heavy concept. He was on the right side . . . wasn't he?

Mr. Grimm continued. "If you are going to stop Basilisk and company then you need to change your tactics."

"What do you mean?" Toby asked, fearing a lecture was coming.

"I've seen your record. Since you were recruited you have survived by brute force and pure luck. It's time for a stealth approach."

Grimm reached behind his seat and pulled out a large black case. He pressed his thumb against a pad and the biometric sensor beeped and unlocked the case. Inside were four black jumpsuits made from a leathery material.

"It's time you started thinking about the bigger picture. You have been behaving like a loose group of individuals, downloading powers without thinking things through. You need to act like a team, using complementary powers and working *together*. These will be your uniforms."

Toby groaned, and Lorna couldn't help but flash a smile. Toby and Pete had been arguing over wearing uniforms. Toby was dead set against it, but Pete had Lorna's vote. Emily sat on the fence over the matter.

"Do we have to? They look so stupid!" Toby moaned.

"This is the very latest in nanofabric weave. The material will automatically take on the same temperature as your surroundings, thus making you invisible to thermal vision or cameras. It will also keep you warm or cool you down and keep you dry. They have a Kevlar weave, which offers resistance to claws, knives, bullets, and mid-range energy weapons. It's fireproof and doesn't need washing or ironing."

"Great," muttered Toby as he examined the one-piece jet-black suit.

"It also comes with matching boots. Nonslip soles. They will automatically fit to your feet, so there is no need for laces."

"No cape?" asked Lorna. She would love to have a

cape, dramatically swirling it around. And it would annoy the heck out of Toby.

"No. Capes are not needed with this clothing system. They're all identical, so you will actually look like a hero team." He fixed his gaze on Toby. "And every team needs a strong leader."

Toby didn't enjoy the scrutiny. He caught Lorna shaking her head and Emily smiling admiringly.

Mr. Grimm broke the uncomfortable silence. "Of course, Hero.com is still off-line so you will have to rely on the irregular powers within you."

He opened a case revealing three small vials of orange liquid. He rolled Lorna's sleeve back to reveal the wristband they all still wore to help control their powers. Grimm ejected the empty vial that contained the teleport power and inserted the new, and slightly larger, cartridge. He repeated the process for Emily and Toby as he spoke.

"Your powers are slowly wearing off and still fluctuating wildly, so I have reprogrammed the wristbands to try and suppress the fluctuations inside you. I have also distilled some raw stealth and defensive powers that we had in storage. It will ensure you can still function as a superteam."

Lorna rolled through the touch screen; a small selection of unfamiliar stick figure icons were available, which she could scroll through left or right.

Welcome to the Jungle

"So without this wristband repressing them, our powers will still randomly fire off," Emily said. "But you're also saying that they could completely vanish at a moment's notice?"

"Correct."

Toby groaned. "So this is a suicide mission?"

"One would hope not."

"Then why give us stealth powers? How about something more useful in an attack?"

"We are literally injecting you with superpowers at this stage. It is not something we would do if we were not desperate. And it is not as though I usually have such superpowers lying around! The Foundation headquarters has been relocated to a classified place, so we can't walk over there and ask to borrow some. By chance these had been donated by a Prime before Hero.com crashed."

"And before he went scurrying into hiding," Toby mumbled.

"No matter what you think, Mr. Wilkinson, you are all regarded as essential assets by the Foundation. You are their only hope."

A rat the size of Pete's foot sniffed around a skeleton shackled to the far wall. Pete couldn't tear his eyes from the rodent: he was terrified of rats. The skeleton had been there for some time, and Pete could not help but notice that its bones had been gnawed. He wondered if the rats had eaten the prisoner alive.

He'd woken up in the small cell; the last thing he remembered was being in his own backyard. He had no idea where he was now. The air was cloying. The walls were crafted from large thick blocks that fitted tightly together and the iron door looked as if it had been added as an afterthought. His wristband had been torn from his arm, leaving an angry red blotch. His hands were bound with unusual cuffs that had a small numeric pad between them. He recognized Emily's description of them as power-dampening handcuffs that Doc Tempest had forced her to wear once when she had been held captive.

The door opened and Trojan stood with her hands on her hips, casting a skeptical look at Pete.

"Come on, kiddo. Somebody wants to speak to you."

For a change, Pete thought bitterly, but he didn't say a word as he stepped from the cell into a narrow, steeply sloping corridor. It was no cooler out there.

Trojan shoved him in the back. "Walk! And no funny business."

Pete couldn't think of any funny quips to throw at her. His thoughts were dark. Abandoned by his friends and facing the prospect of his parents splitting up made him feel as if there was nothing worth returning to. Maybe he should defect to the bad guys for a while. At least he'd be on the winning side. Right now he just didn't care what they were going to do with him.

The stone passage sloped up and Pete got the sense he was walking in a square spiral. It ended at another iron door that was thick with rust. Trojan had to use her shoulder to open this one and gestured for Pete to walk through first. The new room was a stark contrast to what Pete had seen before. It was large, well lit, and paneled with brown tiles. One wall was open and offered a stunning view across a rich jungle canopy. Vividly colored parrots flew past in a large flock.

But Pete's attention was drawn back into the room. Basilisk and Worm stood around a central control column that sat on pneumatic arms, revealing a reclining chair bolted to the floor and surrounded by cables with dry ice drifting from them. Once the column came down it would clearly seal the chair, and its occupant, inside.

"That will be all, Trojan," said Worm. The squat man didn't notice the rude gesture she made behind his back as she left the room, pulling the door closed behind her.

"What is this place?" Pete asked. His dark mood had banished any feelings of fear.

Worm gestured to the chair. "A cryogenic storage chamber. Sit."

Pete ignored him and walked over to the panoramic balcony. Glancing down he could see that he was at the top of a steep stepped pyramid, exactly like the one that he had seen in photographs at Toby's house.

"We're in South America?"

"Central. Mexico, to be precise," said Basilisk. "I'd advise you not to jump. If the fall does not kill you, then the jungle provides many dangers of its own."

"Maybe I'll just fly out of here?"

"Perhaps you could. But with those power-dampening handcuffs on, I very much doubt it." Pete scowled at him. "Now sit down."

Pete still didn't move and he could see that Worm was growing impatient. "What are you going to do with me? I'm no threat. If you think the Enforcers are going to bust through the door or that my friends will be bothered to come and find me, then you're sadly mistaken."

"I know. It seems *nobody* wants you. Except us."

Basilisk effortlessly dragged Pete across the room. Pete shouted and pushed back but without powers it was like fighting an elephant. Basilisk shoved him into the reclining chair and held him in place with one massive palm pushed against Pete's chest, crushing the breath from him. Worm darted forward and pulled restraints across Pete's arms and legs, fastening him in place.

"As I said," grunted Worm, "this is a storage facility. It's where I was entombed for decades. Held in a state of suspended animation. The dimwit Commander

Welcome to the Jungle

Courage thought it would keep me out of the way until the war ended. Then he was going to release me and put me on trial. But the good commander forgot all about me. I would have remained here forever if I hadn't been inadvertently freed by a group of scavenging archaeologists. They accidentally cut the power to my cryogenic chamber when they breached the outer chamber, setting me free."

"What are you going to do to me?" Pete said, now suddenly fearful as Basilisk hovered over him with a nasty-looking implement—all chrome nozzles and serrated edges.

"Take a sample of your DNA," said Basilisk. He placed a nozzle against Pete's arm and squeezed the trigger. Pete yelped. It felt as if he had been bitten. When Basilisk removed the nozzle there was a small circular indentation in Pete's arm, bright red and throbbing.

Basilisk placed the sample in a freezer, then checked some of the old dials on the machine. He tapped one to make the needle move. "We're putting you to sleep. When we bring down the Hero Foundation you will be their *only* Downloader specimen left. We intend to reprogram Hero.com for our own benefit and need to preserve you to see if there will be any unwelcome side effects."

"You're using me as a guinea pig?" Pete futilely struggled against the straps. "Let me out of here!"

Worm gave him a humorless, thin smile. "This will hurt—a lot. For several minutes, as the temperature lowers, it will feel like an icy knife skewering your flesh. But then your brain functions will begin to slow and you'll lose consciousness."

Basilisk slid a curved chrome door half closed. "Just think, you're more useful as a frozen icicle than *anything* else. Sweet dreams."

The column lowered with an ominous thud that reverberated around the chamber, plunging Pete into blackness. A cool breeze replaced the warm air and he heard a sound like gas releasing as the temperature plummeted.

Then he felt as if he'd just fallen into Arctic waters as the cold stabbed his body with such ferocity that he had to scream.

Toby, Lorna, and Emily felt as if they had just arrived in a nightmare. Branches and vines smacked their faces and the dark jungle was alive with hoots, howls, and the sound of a billion insects advancing toward them.

"I hate the jungle!" moaned Lorna.

Hours earlier, Mr. Grimm had taken them to an army base. A small squadron of Enforcers surrounded a sleek black aircraft that reminded Toby of a stretched B-2 stealth bomber. Lorna noticed that the Enforcers were

Welcome to the Jungle

keeping away any inquisitive military personnel. Grimm had informed them that the plane was the next generation of stealth bombers code-named *"Aurora."* It had scramjet technology that enabled it to fly faster than any other military fighter ever had.

"Why can't we teleport there?" asked Toby as they were strapped, chest down, onto specially constructed seats that resembled beds mounted in a circular carousel arrangement, like a ride at the county fair, inside the belly of the aircraft—the bomb bay.

Emily looked terrified as Mr. Grimm explained they would be dropped like bombs over the target area. Their wristbands had been programmed with a limited gliding superpower that would allow them to descend safely.

"We have few samples of teleport charges left outside the Foundation headquarters. This vial is one of a few remaining, and you will need it to return home. And that is *one power* for the four of you—so make sure you are together." He inserted it into Toby's wristband as he continued. "This aircraft will take you in stealthily, invisible to radar and more importantly, to anything Basilisk and company have set up. Remember this is a twofold mission. Stopping Basilisk and his team is your primary goal. No matter how you feel, the rescue mission is of secondary importance. Good luck."

As they were sealed snugly into the bomb bay, which was illuminated with a dim red light, they all agreed that Pete had to be their main concern. Everything else could wait.

They felt very little movement as they took off—until the craft accelerated skyward at such speed they thought the g-forces would tear skin from bone. They heard the engines shriek like banshees and the g-force continued for a full fifteen minutes before they achieved cruising speed.

Toby took the opportunity to interrogate Lorna about missing their dad's exhibition. She mumbled something about forgetting and having previous plans while Emily teased her about going on a date. No names were mentioned, but Toby got the impression that it was somebody from school who he wasn't supposed to know about. Not that he cared.

For two hours they said nothing more, and Toby was surprised to hear Lorna gently snoring. The pilot's voice eventually roused everybody.

"Approaching target area. Cargo deployment in thirty seconds."

Toby assumed that meant them, and wondered if the pilot had known that his cargo was a bunch of teenage superheroes. Probably not.

The pilot began to count down from fifteen. Toby felt a knot of anticipation in his stomach, and heard

Welcome to the Jungle

exclamations from both girls as the bomb bay doors swung open beneath them with a blast of warm air, revealing a moonlit jungle canopy.

Toby barely had time to marvel at the vista before the pilot's count reached "zero" and he felt the bunk he was lying on tip aside, dropping him from the aircraft. The carousel spun around, deploying Emily then Lorna with mechanical precision.

They screamed as they fell, arms and legs flailing as they tried to fly and only remembering at the last moment they had the power to glide. Pushing fear from their minds and focusing on the powers they had, they discovered they could spiral through the air and control the speed of their descent by stretching their arms like wings. It wasn't as much fun as flying, but it was infinitely better than falling.

After ten seconds they had gained enough mastery to look around. The Aurora plane had vanished into the night. The square tops of some ancient Mayan pyramids stood some way off, outlined by the moon. Even in silhouette, Toby recognized the formations as those his father had discovered.

Seconds later they punched through the tree canopy. Branches whipped their faces as they dropped, landing on the jungle floor amid bushes. Lorna was the first to stand, screaming as she frantically swiped at her body, knocking off several large insects.

Toby recalled numerous conversations with his dad about the hazards of field trips in the jungle, although at the time Toby thought they had been nothing more than embellishments of his father's stories to make archaeology sound more adventurous. Leeches drawing blood as you walked across damp ground, hungry jaguars prowling, carnivorous fish, crocodiles, poisonous spiders, scorpions, millipedes, frogs, and deadly plants. Mosquitoes with malaria, insects that buried their young under your skin, and ants with bites so venomous that it felt as if you'd been shot.

Toby decided the best course of action was to keep his mouth shut and not mention anything to alarm the others.

They lost no time in trekking toward the pyramids. After one minute they were soaked with sweat and mosquitoes buzzed irritatingly close to their ears.

"Are you sure that we're heading in the right direction?" Emily asked with concern. They had been walking so long, it seemed that they should have reached their destination by now.

"Totally," said Toby. They followed an animal trail, since it offered the least resistance, and were soon rewarded with large moss-carpeted boulders that showed signs of being carved by man.

"There!" whispered Lorna. She pointed through a narrow break in the trees where the side of a pyramid could just be seen against the sky, which was getting marginally lighter as dawn approached.

They edged forward for a better look, stumbling over yet more carved stones. There were two large symmetrical stepped pyramids stretching out of the jungle.

"Which one is it?" asked Emily.

Toby and Lorna had been forced to watch their father's expedition recordings so much that they felt they had been here before.

"The expedition cleared a trail around the base of the pyramids. But they only had time to explore one tomb before my father was called back," Toby said.

Staring into the darkness, they could just see the trail and noticed that most of the clearing had been done around the farthest structure. Lorna pointed.

"I've seen that entrance on Dad's videos."

Carefully they stepped out on the trail and walked around the base of the nearest pyramid. The stonework was ancient, covered in moss, and weather-beaten. Faded carvings covered every inch. They hurried past and hoped that there were no surveillance cameras watching them. They reached the entrance to the second pyramid and it was as though they had stepped magically into their father's video.

Moonlight reflected from the tarnished seal on the open door. It was metal, something that his father had pointed out was incongruous, as the Mayans had no knowledge of metallurgy, so it must have been added later. It showed a crude serpent, or as Toby had correctly identified, an S-shaped worm placed there by Commander Courage to mark the temporary incarceration of Worm. Toby briefly wondered what terrible accident had befallen the commander to almost kill him and make him forget such a place. It wasn't good to dwell on such dark mysteries.

They peered into the inky blackness. Nothing was visible.

"Wait a minute," said Emily. She looked at her wristband. "Grimm talked about defensive powers, right? Let's see what we have for night vision." She scrolled through the list of irritatingly vague icons on the touch screen and settled on one that showed waves coming from the stick figure's head. "If these are stealth powers, then I doubt it's going to be some kind of laser blast."

She tapped the screen and felt a tingle through her arm as the raw power was transferred via the sensors in her arm.

Lorna took a step back from Emily as her friend's eyes glowed a pale green. It was an unnerving effect.

"I can see!" exclaimed Emily. "Come on, try it. Let's go."

Toby and Lorna chose the same option. The world around them lit up with a pale green light and they could suddenly see into the darkest corner of the chamber ahead. They entered the inner sanctum, and Toby was more than aware that he was tracing his father's steps. The walls were etched with hieroglyphs. Any items that had been decorating the tomb had been taken away and were currently on display in the museum.

"There's nobody here," whispered Emily. "Are you sure this is the right place?"

"Dad only accessed the outer chamber before he had to leave. He said there was a solid stone door preventing them from getting farther inside without a lot of work." Toby had memorized from the display plans in the museum, so he led the way. Now he was glad he'd attended the exhibition. They turned a corner and were confronted by the door to the inner chamber.

Or what was left of it. The corridor was strewn with rubble. The door had been blown apart—from the *inside*. No doubt when Worm had escaped. Beyond, a faint electrical light flickered on the wall and the floor sloped upward.

"I'd say this is definitely it," Toby whispered. His night vision faded as his vision adjusted to the electrical light. "Let's be smart about this. No unnecessary risks. We get Pete, then we get out together. Only then should we decide if we can take Basilisk's team out."

Lorna was impressed with the ease with which Toby was taking charge, although she wouldn't admit it.

They entered the corridor and cautiously walked up. Toby judged that they must have been walking around the perimeter of the pyramid as the passage turned a left-hand corner ahead. Toby peeped around.

The route continued sloping upward and had a single door against the wall, midway, before it turned yet another left-hand corner, spiraling up the structure. They cautiously passed the door and saw a dingy cell beyond the narrow bars.

"Empty," said Toby, who had hoped they could have sprung Pete from the cell quickly and easily.

They reached the next corner. As Toby was about to step out he felt Emily pull him back and push him against the wall, clamping a hand over his mouth.

"Listen," she whispered.

It was strange to Toby to have Emily so close. This wasn't the time to think about girls—*especially* Emily. Toby shook the thoughts away. He strained to listen instead. Arguing voices drifted from another room halfway along the passage.

"You killed him!" said a female voice.

"I thought you were going to shoot him!" barked an angry male voice.

Lorna rolled through the options on her wristband looking for a blank icon square. She hoped that she had invisibility; that was the ultimate stealth power. No luck.

Welcome to the Jungle

"Wait here," said Toby. "I'll scout ahead."

Before they could argue, Toby gingerly tiptoed toward the door and pressed himself flat against the wall. He was annoyed at himself as he couldn't get the *Mission Impossible* theme song from his head, and regretted having watched the movies with Pete a couple of days earlier. He risked a peek around the corner, expecting to witness a scene of torture.

Instead he saw the backs of Viral and Trojan. They had their feet up and were playing a PlayStation game, shooting digital foes on a tiny screen. Toby swallowed his relieved laugh—it was nice to know that villains were people too. He crept past the opening and checked that they hadn't heard him, then waved for the others to follow him.

"Look out!" screamed Trojan.

Lorna froze in the open doorway, convinced she was caught. A quick check revealed that Trojan was still referring to the game.

The trio advanced up the sloping corridor, and judging by the fact that each turn was shorter than the last, Toby knew they must be close to the apex.

So far, so good, he thought. He'd expected things to be much more difficult than they had been. But then, an iron door blocked the passage ahead, and behind it, they could hear the low thrum of machinery and muffled voices. Although the words were indistinguishable, both Basilisk and Worm were easily identifiable. Shadows moved on the floor.

Toby studied the heavy door. Without any energy weapons or superstrength there was no way they could charge their way through, and he realized that they were effectively trapped at the top of the ancient Mayan pyramid with two dangerous supervillains ahead of them and another two behind.

Toby scrolled through the superpowers on his wristband and hoped there was *something* they could use to save Pete.

Exit Strategy

Basilisk stared at Worm and, not for the first time, pondered how he was going to get rid of the irritating little man once they'd triumphed with the plan. Aside from his brief capture, which, in fact, had turned out to be a blessing now that they had a Downloader in captivity, the plan had been flawless. Hero.com was still down, the Primes who ran it were in hiding, and the Hero Foundation was an open target—or would be once he had located it, of course.

But time was beginning to turn against them.

The virus he had inserted into the system at Goonhilly had been state-of-the-art and caused more damage than he'd thought possible. But Basilisk knew it was only a matter of time before the Foundation's nonsuper technicians got Hero.com working again—and it was taking him longer than he'd anticipated to access the Foundation satellites. If he didn't do that soon then he'd be back to square one. When he had voiced his concerns to Worm, the little man instantly began to worry.

"Perhaps it is time for the Council to step in to help us topple the Foundation?" he whined.

Basilisk flicked a glance at the suspended animation pod that entrapped the boy.

"No doubt they would destroy the Foundation," Basilisk growled, "and Hero.com with it. Then what good would it do to hand the power to them?"

"Asking for help is better than failure! Why should we struggle in the final steps when the Council would be all too willing to—"

Basilisk raised his voice. "This is bigger than your petty drive to avenge yourself on Commander Courage. Think of the bigger picture for once! We will have *our own* superpower Web site. Besides, the Council has no love for me after I tried to overturn them. They would kill me in the process." He caught Worm's calculating expression. "And *you* for harboring me for so long. I'm beginning to think that you're getting cold feet."

Worm shook his head. "Not at all." In truth the desire for revenge on the Hero Foundation creator was something that burned through him. "But instead of action we hide away in this prison," spat Worm, who didn't have the vocabulary to describe how much he hated the pyramid, jungle, and entire country.

Neither man noticed a subtle movement under the door. It looked as though somebody had pushed a sheet of paper underneath—a paper printed with a picture of Toby.

But in fact it was Toby himself.

He was wafer thin, and pulled himself through the narrow gap under the doorway. It was an unusual experience to be so thin, and he found it difficult to grip the stone floor to drag himself into the room.

Basilisk continued. "As I have explained, we leave the boy here and proceed to phase two. Thanks to our infiltration of the satellite station in Britain, I *know* which satellite the Foundation is using to transmit the powers. We need to get to that satellite so Viral can act."

"About time! All he's done is make the place smell with his rank odor. After all the effort we went through to release him you'd think he'd at least take a shower. So what can he do that's so important?"

"Once you open up the system for him, Viral can insert a malicious code directly into the satellite to pinpoint the location the Foundation is transmitting from. Then he can knock their security systems off-line so we can perform our final assault."

"At last, some action."

"Once he has inserted his virus it won't matter if they bring Hero.com back online, since we'll control the satellite!"

"Why does everything you do seem complicated?"

"Because nothing in life is easy! Not if it's worth

doing. My plan is foolproof and *will* see us victorious!" *With you in a box*, Basilisk added silently.

Toby was now through the door and he dragged himself behind the central steel column. He stood upright, careful to keep his paper-thin edge toward the villains. For a frightening moment, he thought he caught Worm glancing over, but the villain didn't seem to notice him.

"And what about the other two? I don't like them."

Basilisk was secretly plotting to use Viral and Trojan to assault Villain.net as well, but that was a future plan that didn't concern Worm. "After this is over you can deal with them." Basilisk resisted laughing out loud—Trojan and Viral would tear Worm apart.

Toby looked at the machine's controls in front of him. He had been expecting to find Pete tied up, and was shocked to see his friend's face on a monitor. Heart sensors steadily beeped indicating he was alive, and Toby somehow knew he must be contained in the column in front of him.

"Very well. I allow you to continue," said Worm.

"Most generous," purred Basilisk, who wanted nothing more than to pulverize the little fiend into dust.

"I will charge up the *Nematode* so we can proceed with the second phase."

Toby watched as Worm strode toward the panoramic opening at the top of the pyramid, which wasn't visible from the outside, camouflaged by a holographic screen.

Exit Strategy

Worm suddenly dissolved into fine sandlike grains that cascaded down the side of the pyramid, reforming into the villain once the grains reached the jungle floor.

Toby grinned. If they waited for the bad guys to leave they would have no problem freeing Pete. Basilisk spun around and headed for the door.

That was when Toby saw the flaw in his plan. He had no time to shout out before Basilisk yanked open the door.

Lorna and Emily froze when they saw the villain. Basilisk stopped in his tracks too, stunned to see them.

Chaos erupted.

"Intruders!" he roared.

Toby took a step forward, intending to distract Basilisk, but then noticed a large red button amid the old dials on the control panel. It was such an obvious button to press, and Toby rationalized that it would probably have been a stylish design sixty-odd years ago when the machine had been constructed. With the villain momentarily distracted this was his chance to release Pete.

He hit the button.

An alarm squawked out, drowning Basilisk's voice. Yellow warning lights rotated on the cryogenic chamber and an icy high-pressure mist shot out of the machine.

Basilisk's eyes blazed malevolently. Both Emily and

Lorna screamed in agony as they felt their skin tighten-ing across their bodies. The sensation vanished the moment Basilisk broke eye contact to twist around to see the dry ice flood the room behind him.

"Who's there?" he yelled in obvious confusion.

Emily and Lorna turned to retreat but froze when they saw Trojan and Viral running up the corridor behind them. The villains slowed their pace when they saw the intruders were trapped.

Viral grinned evilly. "Lost, little girls?"

Lorna grabbed Emily and shouted something. Toby saw all this through the dry ice filling the room. He watched as Emily and Lorna stabbed their wristbands and then vanished in a cloud of smoke that mixed with the vapors in the room.

Basilisk turned and ran toward the console, still obliv-ious to Toby's presence. Toby circled around him and slammed the door closed, pulling a heavy bar across it to prevent Viral and Trojan from entering the room.

Basilisk spun around and finally noticed Toby, who stood like a two-dimensional cartoon character. Behind, the cryogenic chamber rose to reveal an unconscious Pete strapped to the chair, covered in a sheen of ice.

"You don't give up, do you?" Basilisk snarled when he recognized him.

Toby was well aware that he was on his own. Emily and Lorna must have teleported away. Half of him resented the fact they'd left him on his own while the other half understood that they had been trapped with only one escape route.

"I just came for my friend, Basilisk," said Toby, raising his wafer-thin hands for a fight even though he looked ridiculous. A passing thought made him wonder if a single punch from the supervillain would tear a hole through him. That would surely kill him.

"Then come and get him, boy."

Toby took a step forward and wondered how he could avoid the villain's gaze. Trojan suddenly appeared in the room with a flourish of her cape; Viral walked out from the folds of the material as it swished around the girl. Trojan wasn't wearing her mask, and Toby thought for a second she looked very attractive, until she gave him a cruel smile. He was outnumbered.

And he was probably going to die.

Emily and Lorna reappeared with a sucking noise. They felt dizzy from their quick escape. They were standing on the broad flat top of the pyramid opposite the one they had just fled. Dawn illuminated the jungle. Lorna was momentarily struck by how beautiful the landscape looked.

Moments before, she and Emily had been examining the options on their wristbands and thought they'd identified one that could be useful—when Basilisk had opened the door. Once the other villains appeared behind them they had little choice but to select the new power, and to hope.

Their bodies atomized in a cloud with a sensation that felt like being tickled all over. Although their bodies were no longer larger than a particle of smoke, they could still see around them. They zoomed past Basilisk and circled the chamber like ghosts before spotting the opening outside. They shot through and banked across to the pyramid opposite just as the power wore off.

Emily pointed back at the pyramid. A solid-looking wall was blocking the opening they had escaped from. She stared for a couple of seconds, and then noticed the image glitch as if it was a looped video image.

"It's a fake wall! A hologram or something."

"We've got to go back and get Toby."

"We can't fight with just defensive powers."

"What do we do?"

"Give me a second, Lorn. I have an idea."

Toby grunted in pain. His power abruptly wore off and his entire body reinflated like an expanding balloon. It felt like being punched all over.

Trojan watched in surprise. "Nice trick."

"Thanks." He gave her what he thought was a charming smile, before remembering the danger he was in.

"Can we just kill him already?" snarled Viral.

Basilisk nodded. "Yes, he's of no use to us."

Toby took a step back and felt the iron door blocking his path. Viral opened his mouth to say something snotty.

Then he was blasted off his feet by a fireball that slammed him against the ancient Mayan wall. Trojan and Basilisk spun around to see Emily and Lorna swoop through the archway. Emily landed next to Pete and immediately began unfastening his restraints. Lorna unleashed another fireball between Trojan and Basilisk—forcing them to leap aside.

"Tobe! We are *leaving*!" she screamed.

Toby didn't have time to ponder where they had found these powers; instead he darted forward and helped Emily free Pete.

The three downed villains were all trying to rise at the same time. An energy blast erupted from Basilisk's hands—Lorna darted aside as the beam punched a jagged hole in the ancient brickwork. She retaliated with a fireball that hit Basilisk firmly in his chest and rolled him into Viral. She spun around with another fireball aimed at Trojan—but it exploded harmlessly against Trojan's cape as she pulled it up.

Pete was a dead weight and still unconscious when

Emily and Toby pulled him from the chair. His skin was cold to the touch, but they had no time to check him over.

Lorna dropped to the floor. "Oh no! My flying's out!"

Toby and Emily dragged Pete across to the opening and Lorna smashed the cuffs from his hands before sending another fireball into the room—this time targeting the cryogenic column. It exploded into chunks, forcing everybody to duck.

"We're trapped again," Emily commented with forced calm.

Toby looked down the steep, stepped side of the pyramid. It was a long way down, and a difficult climb. Without a flying power they were stuck.

"What was your plan for getting out?"

"I hoped we could still fly," said Lorna.

An energy blast from Basilisk clipped the wall next to them, stone shards cutting Toby's face. Trojan and Viral joined him, wiping debris off their clothes.

"Why don't you jump and make it easier on yourselves," snarled Viral. "Because when I'm finished with you there's not going to be much of you left."

Toby advanced as Basilisk raised his arms to fire again. He hit an icon on the wristband that he'd been dying to try out. There was a bright flash—and then there were suddenly ten Tobys facing the villains. Each duplicate looked at the other and smiled.

Exit Strategy

Basilisk fired at the target that *had been* the real Toby. The duplicate vanished with a popping noise.

"What is this?" snarled Basilisk, clearly at a loss as the army of Tobys advanced.

The real Toby had been teleported several yards to the side as the duplicates appeared—it was like the old trick of trying to find a ball under a cup. He still had no attack powers, but hoped Basilisk didn't know that. And when he spoke, his eight other images spoke too.

"Time for *you* to run. I have nine times the power right here!"

Viral kicked out at one image—it popped away like a soap bubble.

"Unlucky," grinned Toby.

"If you could attack us," said Basilisk slowly, "then you would have done so already. You can't do it, can you?"

The expression on the eight Tobys' faces betrayed what he was feeling. Then he heard Emily shout out.

"Toby! Let's go!" She and Lorna had picked Pete up between them.

The eight Tobys turned and sprinted for Emily. Toby could feel Basilisk unleash a blast of energy behind him and the stone slabs on the floor were torn away like a rug. He flailed forward and landed at Emily's feet, flat on his face.

She thumbed her wristband and a spherical shield

enveloped the four of them. Basilisk fired again. The blast ricocheted from the shield.

"You won't leave here alive!" bellowed Basilisk in fury, and his eyes seemed to explode in a fluorescent blue flash.

Toby screamed as he felt his skin begin to harden; the moisture was being sucked from it. Despite the pain, he had a sudden idea. Like a hamster, he pushed the curved inside of the ball—and the four of them rolled off the edge of the pyramid!

One time on vacation, Toby had tried an extreme sport known as zorbing, which involved being strapped inside a giant inflated ball and kicked down a hill. It was an exhilarating experience. And one they were copying now.

The energy ball bounced recklessly down the stepped pyramid slope, gaining momentum. Everybody inside was jostled around—heads butted and bodies painfully clashed.

Basilisk dived straight down in pursuit. Unable to fly, both Trojan and Viral stopped at the edge and watched as the energy ball bounced from the bottom step and vaulted into the jungle.

With little else to do, Toby screamed as they pinballed through the jungle, bouncing from tree to tree in sudden direction changes. At one point they burst into a clearing where Worm was inspecting the fuselage of the *Nematode*. The diminutive villain barely had time to hit the deck as the energy ball slammed into the side of his machine and rebounded into the thick jungle. Seconds later Basilisk flew through the clearing at breakneck speed, following the sphere in a wide arc.

Just as Toby thought he was going to be sick, the ball made a final bounce—and didn't seem to hit the ground again. He became aware they were falling from a great height. . . .

They had dropped from a cliff edge and plummeted to one of the few rivers on the Yucatan peninsula. Mr. Grimm's briefing rattled through his mind at light speed. Worm had been imprisoned in Yucatan because the whole peninsula was built on limestone. It might have been a soft rock but it was dense enough to foil his powers. The limestone meant that there were few lakes or rivers on the main peninsula because the rocks acted like a sponge, forming giant cenotes—or sink-holes—that held the water. What few rivers there were led out to the ocean and were infested with crocodiles.

Toby remembered all of that as they fell toward the river—just as Emily's power died and the shield vanished.

They landed with an enormous splash, and Toby felt himself being dragged toward the bottom of the river. He frantically kicked toward the surface and emerged, spluttering, next to Emily. Lorna was not too far away.

"Where's Pete?" he shouted, spitting out a mouthful of water.

Pete suddenly popped to the surface, gulping air and yelling so much that Toby couldn't help smiling; at least it meant he was alive.

A gentle current tugged at them.

"Make for the shore!" Emily shouted.

Before she could move, Basilisk shot through the trees and hovered over the wide river, spotting the figures immediately. He was so angry that he didn't even pause to deliver a mocking epitaph. He just fired his energy bolt straight at them.

Emily and Toby submerged and saw the blast smash into the water above them, creating a torrent of bubbles. The residual force from the energy rippled across the water and struck Lorna. She immediately fell limp.

Toby kicked toward her and broke the surface just as Basilisk fired again. The bolt landed wide, allowing Toby to support Lorna above the water. She looked pale, but was coming around. Toby scrambled for her wristband to activate the shield she had used. The pad was missing.

"Where is it?"

Lorna was too weak to answer. Toby glanced up to see Basilisk swooping low—and Emily was right in his path.

Pete had seen this too. The suspended animation had left him feeling groggy and his joints felt as if they were still frozen solid, even bathed in the relatively warm river. He snarled in anger and thrust his hand at Basilisk, not really knowing if anything would happen—but remembering one of the first times he had ever used his powers.

A cone of ice shot out from his hand—and smashed into Basilisk with such force he was propelled backward. Pete released his rage in one long scream—something he had wanted to do since he discovered his parents were splitting up, his home had been destroyed, and he'd been kidnapped—and the scream didn't stop until Basilisk was trapped in a huge ball of ice that plummeted into the water.

The effort made Pete so weak that he no longer had the strength to keep himself afloat. Seconds later he felt arms around him and he was dragged to the river-bank. Only when he felt the pebbly riverbed beneath him did he risk looking around to see who his savior was. Emily beamed back at him.

"Good to see you again," she said. Then they both glanced up to see the bizarre sight of a mini iceberg drifting past in the tropical jungle river, with Basilisk at the core.

The heroes regrouped on dry land, fighting for breath and grinning from ear to ear. Even in the early morning the humid atmosphere was oppressive, but the dip had cooled them down.

Toby helped Lorna sit upright; her arms and legs were numb from where the blast had ricocheted into her. But she assured Toby that the feeling was coming back.

"What just happened?" Pete asked, rubbing his joints to improve his circulation.

Toby filled him in on events. Then Lorna and Emily told them how Emily had remembered that the wristbands were controlling the powers stored inside them by *suppressing* them. By tearing off Lorna's wristband she had allowed the wild powers inside her to manifest—a risk, since they had no idea if she would be able to use the powers effectively, and losing the wristband would leave Lorna defenseless.

For his part, Pete had told them about the night with Basilisk, his parents, and the attack on his house. The others listened in guilty silence and gushed apologies once he had finished. Pete didn't respond. How could he, since he blamed them too? He first wondered if it was an aftereffect of being frozen alive, but then realized something had snapped inside him. He now knew the only person he could rely on was himself. He wasn't part of the team anymore. He'd be better off alone and would demand his own access to Hero.com.

But he kept these thoughts quiet. He'd talk to the others once this whole mess had been resolved.

Exit Strategy

Toby knew they still had to face Worm and the others, but there was some good news. "At least we got rid of that stone-faced supergoon, right?"

"Wrong!"

They spun around to see Basilisk rising from the water, sodden and disheveled. Lumps of ice clung to his cape and he tore his hood down, revealing a rapidly decaying face that might have been recognizable if his regeneration powers had been working. As he reached the bank, he raised a hand and shot an energy bolt at Pete.

Pete found himself pitched sideways as Emily crashed into him—taking the brunt of the blast.

"Em!" screamed Lorna—but she froze as Basilisk raised his hand toward her.

"Stop!" he commanded. "Or you'll die like your friend!"

Pete gritted his teeth and shot out his hand.

Nothing happened. He stared at his fingers, dumbstruck. He tried again and this time Basilisk burst into laughter.

"Your powers are nothing more than random residuals of the mighty Hero.com! Without the Web site they are withering, and will soon fade to nothing."

Pete stood to face Basilisk as he approached. He tried another power—nothing.

"Come on, boy. Take your best shot."

Basilisk opened his arms to provide the largest possible target. "Strike me down!"

Instead Pete delivered a kick to Basilisk's groin that would have toppled an elephant. Basilisk didn't flinch.

"You're useless. All of you. The Foundation's little foot soldiers have achieved nothing. How the mighty have fallen."

He roughly pushed Pete to the ground.

"In fact I have no need to kill you. Why bother? I will let the jungle take you."

Toby had been fingering his wristband. He knew the powers on it were defensive or stealth ones—but after a glance at Emily's prone body, there was no way he could let Basilisk walk away. He stabbed one button and felt the power transfer.

"We're going to bring you down, Basilisk," he shouted.

Basilisk gave him a questioning look and opened his mouth to speak just as Toby extended his arms and wondered exactly what he'd selected.

His arms continued to extend like elastic and punched Basilisk across the jaw. Basilisk stumbled backward, not from the blow, but out of surprise. Toby's arms snapped back to normal and he tried a kick.

Basilisk's eyes glowed blue as Toby's leg shot out several feet and booted Basilisk forcefully into the river. Pete and Lorna joined in the attack by hurling rocks at

Basilisk. A few drew blood as they struck his head and the water around him turned pink.

"Enough!" screamed Basilisk. "Time for you to join your friend!"

He stood, using one stonelike arm to shield his bleeding forehead, and raised the other to fire.

There was a sudden explosion of water around Basilisk. Toby thought one of the others had unleashed a power against him. But then he saw a darker shape in the water—a huge crocodile sprang from the river, jaws open as it sensed blood. The splashing water obscured the brunt of the violence—but they all saw the jaws clamp across Basilisk's chest as he was dragged down into the water.

Lorna screamed in horror. Pete took the chance to run across to Emily's body and kneel by her.

"Lorn, we're getting out of here!" Toby shouted as he grabbed Lorna's arm, tearing her away from the river.

Basilisk was putting up a fight. He resurfaced, raising a stone arm and deflecting the crocodile's powerful bite. With his other hand he unleashed an energy bolt that heaved the beast from the river and threw it back into the water with a mighty splash. Basilisk roared with primeval victory.

But he didn't see the three other prehistoric hunters charge behind him. One clamped around his arm like a rabid dog, while the other bit his torso.

Unable to watch any longer, Lorna and Toby joined their friends.

"Hold on to me!" Toby instructed, and selected the teleport option from the wristband.

The last thing he saw was Basilisk being dragged into the churning water by ravenous crocodiles—an energy blast ripping one of the animals apart just as another came to take its place.

Then the heroes teleported out of Mexico.

The Beginning of a Nightmare

The hard bucket seat was probably the most uncomfortable thing Toby had ever sat on, but he still found himself nodding off to sleep. His head slipped from where his arm propped it up, jolting him back awake. He looked around the drab waiting room and saw that Lorna had finally cried herself to sleep. Pete lay across several seats with his back to them all, but Toby was pretty sure he'd heard sniffling coming from him, too.

The auto-teleport device had been preprogrammed to bring them to a small, empty office in the middle of an industrial estate. A plump woman had watched them appear in midair, and smiled pleasantly, as though this kind of thing happened all the time. Which, for her, it probably did.

It turned out to be a Hero Foundation safe house, disguised as a plumbing supply distribution office. She immediately checked Emily for a pulse, and assured everybody that she was still alive. Barely. Then the woman called for an ambulance. Toby was surprised when a few minutes later an air ambulance appeared and ferried them to a private Foundation hospital, one of many they were told were located in almost every country around the world.

Emily had been taken right away on a stretcher while Mr. Grimm greeted the others and took them to a private office where he debriefed them. They all found it difficult to answer Mr. Grimm's barrage of questions. The man didn't express even a modicum of emotion when they described Emily being struck down. If anything, he was annoyed that they had left without stopping Basilisk.

Fighting fatigue, Toby snapped at him. It was clear they didn't have the experience or even the range of powers to fight four seasoned supervillains, one of whom was so dangerous that he'd been in Diablo Island's *maximum* security wing. It was time the Primes came out of hiding to help.

"That won't happen. Even Chameleon has vanished," Mr. Grimm replied.

Toby gasped in surprise. "What happened?"

Mr. Grimm shrugged. "He risked his life and it seems he paid the price. As I feared, the balance has been broken. Anarchy is slowly breaking out on a global scale."

Silence filled the room. Toby felt sick. Chameleon had been his mentor and the only Prime, aside from

The Beginning of a Nightmare

Mr. Grimm, who had spared any time to talk to them. He glanced at Lorna and Pete. They looked crestfallen. Mr. Grimm turned on a TV in the corner of the room. It played a muted news channel, but the images said it all. Reporters stood in front of burning buildings and streets trashed from terrible fights. Mr. Grimm took a sip of water, then steepled his fingers as he continued.

"In the last twenty-four hours virtually every city around the world has experienced a supercrime attack. They're mostly high-profile robberies and kidnappings. Every attack has the Council of Evil's signature. Global military forces are on high alert and of course, the public is being kept in the dark as much as possible. It's all being blamed on gang warfare and terrorists." A frown creased his smooth brow. "Which was difficult when the Statue of Liberty was destroyed and the president of the United States kidnapped by the Hunter."

Toby rubbed his eyes as he saw the image on TV: the iconic Lady Liberty was lying in pieces. What could *they* possibly do to strike back without stable superpowers?

"A small detachment of Enforcers has been deployed to try to round up Basilisk's gang. Hopefully you have weakened them enough. But if they fail, then it falls to you to stop them."

HERO.CÜM

Toby shook his head. "So you keep saying. But there's nothing we can do!"

"You're a team. We each have our part to play. That was the understanding when you signed up for Hero.com. That formed a contract of trust, honesty, and loyalty."

"Ha! Right!" snapped Pete. "I think you have the wrong group for that. They're qualities we don't have." Pete shot Mr. Grimm the sort of dirty look that he usually reserved for the backs of bullies, and once again Toby wondered how much Pete's parents' split was affecting his friend. "We're a terrible team. We're just a group of kids who don't know what we're doing! I even wonder if *you* know what you're doing—you put Toby in charge! What about me? I read all the comic books, I know we're supposed to coordinate our attacks and work together. Instead we're just running around improvising every time there's a problem! You keep yapping on about a balance when the truth is more like every man for himself. Otherwise you'd be risking your own life instead of ours."

The telephone rang, breaking the tense atmosphere. Mr. Grimm swooped it up. He didn't say a word before replacing the handset.

"Emily is conscious. The doctors here are skilled in assisting hyperenergy-related wounds and have begun a regeneration process for her. She'll be as good as new in a few hours. You should take this time to rest."

The Beginning of a Nightmare

"Can we go home?" Toby asked eagerly. Out of the corner of his eye he saw Pete go rigid.

"No." Mr. Grimm saw their expressions, and held up a slim hand in reassurance. "Your families are perfectly safe. But you still have a mission to finish if the Enforcers fail."

An orderly led them to the waiting room where they were given some food in sterile plastic trays. Lorna didn't like it; it tasted as if the flavor had been sucked from every molecule. She had retrieved her cell phone from Pete, and despite the freezing and dunking it had received, it had dried out and worked perfectly, even if the screen was now cracked. She was delighted to see that she had several voice-mail messages.

Lorna left the room to make a call and answered Toby's questioning glance with: "Don't worry; I'm not calling Mom and Dad."

"So who are you calling?"

"A friend," she mumbled, and quickly exited.

"Boyfriend," Pete stated bluntly.

Toby didn't feel like talking to Pete after his outburst. He stared at the ceiling and prayed that the Enforcers could capture or kill Worm and the others. If not, he and his friends were supposed to save the world from complete anarchy.

Toby couldn't shake the feeling that the world was doomed.

* * *

Trojan and Viral swapped uneasy glances as they were rocked in their red velvet seats aboard the *Nematode*. Worm was at the controls and they could see nothing but black earth passing the bug-eyed windows and hear the occasional clang of rocks striking the bronze hull. They glanced back at Basilisk, who was strapped flat on the floor, like a piece of cargo.

"They're not following," Worm declared with some relief.

Less than an hour earlier Trojan and Viral had escaped from the burning control room by climbing down the side of the pyramid. They had rejoined Worm in the clearing and watched as an angry orange fireball ripped off the top of the pyramid.

"There goes our HQ," said Trojan wistfully. "I kind of liked it."

"Good riddance to my prison," snapped Worm, who had only used the facility after Basilisk had convinced him that they required a base for operations.

With her powers recharged, Trojan had volunteered to search for Basilisk in the jungle. Quantum shifting on her own meant she could make more trips than if she had to take others. After fifteen minutes of fruitless hunting she had stepped out on a riverbank and discovered Basilisk washed up and surrounded by

The Beginning of a Nightmare

several dead crocodiles. She had carefully approached, aware that there were more of the reptiles lurking in the water.

Basilisk stirred, although he was covered in wounds and had lost a lot of blood. Sensing new prey, one crocodile leaped from the water and sprinted across the shore at a startling speed. Trojan had thrown her cape across Basilisk and they both reappeared next to the *Nematode*.

But then automatic gunfire had torn a line across the clearing between Viral and Trojan. Two black UH-60 Black Hawk helicopters circled around with Enforcers hanging from the doorways.

"Those stupid kids must have led them right to us!" Worm shouted as he raced toward the *Nematode*. Viral was several paces behind him as more gunshots peppered the tunneling machine.

"You bring the Big Guy in!" he called to Trojan.

She was about to respond when she was forced to throw her cape up as a solid shield, as bullets rained down around her.

"I can't!" she screamed. "You'll have to help me."

Viral hesitated. His own skin was too valuable to risk on saving Basilisk, but the villain *had* masterminded his escape. And his plan for toppling the Hero Foundation was brilliant. Viral was many bad things, but he was not disloyal. Plus he was feeling attracted to Trojan, even though he knew that he didn't stand a chance. What did he expect with a name like Viral? He was already thinking about rebranding himself once this was over.

He sprinted back to Trojan. "Grab his arm."

They grunted with effort. Basilisk was much heavier than he looked, and both villains only had average strength. The Black Hawks hovered at opposite ends of the clearing as Worm powered up the *Nematode*.

"Hurry!" he called.

Viral saw muzzle flashes from the Enforcers and heard the gunfire over the sound of the thunderous helicopter rotors. Trojan threw her cape in front of them both to act as a shield.

"They've pinned us down," she warned. "And my shield won't last forever."

Viral nodded—then jumped from behind the protective cape. In the two seconds he had to spare, he noticed that the Enforcers were all wearing bright yellow biohazard suits that protected them from his powers, but made them colorful targets.

Viral flicked his hands and a mist shot out, splattering across one of the Black Hawks. For a moment nothing happened, and he could see the Enforcers readying themselves for another strafing run. Then an orange patch appeared on the helicopter's hull and quickly spread across the machine in every direction. The crew

The Beginning of a Nightmare

inside looked around as the metal exterior started to dissolve in a rusty hue.

In seconds the aircraft's entire fuselage crumbled to rust—including most of the engine and rotors. The men inside found themselves sitting on seats that were no longer attached to anything—and fell into the jungle in a fine particle cloud of oxidized metals.

Viral turned to the other helicopter—but it sharply banked out of sight. With a grin he helped lug Basilisk into the *Nematode*. As soon as Trojan sealed the door, Worm accelerated and the machine burrowed beneath the earth.

Emily was sitting up in the hospital bed, cramming more chocolate into her mouth. The others sat around her. On Pete's suggestion, they had all chipped in what little money they carried and bought Emily the get-well chocolates. Not that she needed them. Her cuts and bruises had vanished and she declared herself ready to leap back into action, until Pete whispered that she should play out her injuries a little longer as they were all tired and couldn't face another mission outside.

Toby looked around the well-appointed ward with curiosity. Most of the curtains were drawn around the beds, so he had no idea who occupied them, but the ward was full. The nurses all wore pristine white uniforms with the Hero Foundation logo embroidered on them, and they busied themselves moving from bed to bed.

"What did they do to you?" Pete asked with curiosity.

Emily shrugged. "I dunno. When I woke up I had an IV in me, like that one."

She pointed across to another bed, which had an IV suspended from a stand feeding the patient just beyond the curtains. The fluid inside was dirty green and Pete swore it was glowing slightly.

"Must be a regeneration power," he mused.

"Whatever it is, it cured me. Healed my wounds, the doctors said. Apparently if you hadn't gotten me here so fast, I would have been a goner."

Pete mumbled, getting tongue-tied. "Yeah. For a minute there I was, uh, worried . . . you know . . . that . . . "

Emily beamed at him and he turned away as red as a beet. This was the first time any of them had been this close to death.

"I think we should stop doing all of this," said Lorna, resolutely avoiding Toby's glower. "It's not right that we should be risking our lives. Like Pete said, we're terrible."

"I said we were a terrible team," snapped Pete. "It doesn't mean I don't enjoy having the powers. Better than sitting at home staring at the wall and listening to constant—"

He shut up before he said *arguing*.

The Beginning of a Nightmare

"It's not worth dying for," Lorna said firmly.

Toby stood up; he was angry at his sister's defeatist attitude. "Then what is? We've been told we're *it*. Without us out there trying to stop these villains destroying the Foundation, the world as we know it will be overrun!"

Lorna shook her head. "I don't believe that."

"You've seen the news! How can you ignore what's going on?"

"I don't believe that we're the *only* ones who can stop this. I mean, who are we? We're just a bunch of—"

"Kids?" said Toby. Lorna nodded. "I don't care what Pete said." He pointed a finger at Pete. "He's wrong! We've been selected to have an opportunity, a duty, with these powers. And I think we should be out there helping as best we can."

Lorna opened her mouth to argue, but stopped when she felt Emily's hand on hers.

"I have to agree, Lorn. Like Pete said, we enjoy doing it. Otherwise why bother, right? And we're just getting the hang of all this, so we're not going to be the best team there is. Not yet. But if we keep working together," she glanced at Toby, "and have strong leadership, then I know we'll be fine. Lorn, you said that you'd like to be famous with all these powers. How much more famous do you think you could get then as the girl who saved the world?"

Despite their frustration, Toby and Pete couldn't

help but smile. Trust Emily to touch Lorna's vanity button.

"Em's right," said Pete. "Look at it this way, none of us died. In fact, Emily doesn't have a scratch on her!"

Toby grinned, glad to see the old Pete back. "Exactly. No matter what, we're in this together, as a *team*."

"For now," Pete said firmly.

The smile slid off Toby's face. He'd been wrong. There was an unmistakable coolness to Pete's attitude. He noticed that Emily had spotted it too but remained silent.

Lorna looked at the three of them and reluctantly nodded. "Okay. Count me in before we all start fighting again."

Toby was relieved the argument had been stopped. "Don't forget, Lorn, at the end of the day, we're super-heroes. We're special."

"Touching," Mr. Grimm said from the end of the bed. Everybody jumped in surprise. They hadn't seen or heard him approach. "It seems Miss Harper is fit and ready for active duty, is she not?"

Emily felt so good she couldn't stop herself from grinning as she threw a mock salute.

The humor bypassed Grimm. "Excellent. Then you're ready for more bad news. The Enforcers have failed. It's now all up to you."

The Beginning of a Nightmare

* * *

Basilisk knew that he was dying, but he could prevent that. What really annoyed him most was the lousy timing of it. Aside from the brief hiccups, the scheme had gone according to plan, and the destruction of the Hero Foundation was within reach.

Before the meddlesome Downloaders had rescued their friend, Basilisk and Worm had been assessing the trouble across the globe. The organized attacks were a clear sign that the Council of Evil was taking advantage of the collapse of Hero.com to maximize chaos.

And for Basilisk, that was all for the best.

Once they had seized control of the Hero Foundation he would get Viral and Trojan to dispose of Worm. Then he could reinstate Hero.com under his own control, although he'd have to think of a suitable name change, and use it to recruit cannon fodder to strike at the Council of Evil.

If he lived that long.

Since his encounter with the schoolboy Jake Hunter, almost a month earlier, Basilisk had been feeling increasingly weak. His normal regeneration skills would have patched him up in twenty-four hours after Worm had taken him off his crumbling island. But he had been suffering for far too long now and suspected that it was time for him to regenerate again. Basilisk healed, at a genetic level, by stealing DNA from a victim to rebuild his own. He had done this to Jake Hunter, but now Basilisk knew he needed to do it again. He couldn't take it from another Prime, such as Trojan, as that would cause severe reactions with his own superpowers.

When he came around aboard the *Nematode* he found the others looking at him with concern. Not for his well-being, of course, but because without the plan Basilisk carried in his head, they didn't know what to do next. Plus, Trojan had started wondering aloud if they'd all be in trouble with the Council of Evil for aiding and abetting a known fugitive. That left them in a diffi-cult position.

Basilisk's breathing was laborious, and through cracked lips he insisted they return to the pyramid to retrieve something they had stored there.

Trojan entered the ruins while Viral kept a lookout. It didn't take her long to find what Basilisk wanted. It was a small refrigeration unit that had been severely dented in the explosion, but its contents were still cold and intact.

She returned to the *Nematode* and Basilisk eagerly tore open the box and pulled out the frosted sterile containment flask. The flask opened with a pressurized hiss. Held inside was the small, perfectly preserved sample they had taken from Pete to study.

The others watched as Basilisk held it in the palm of

The Beginning of a Nightmare

his hand. His own skin started to rapidly grow around the sample, absorbing it into his body. It was as though he was a genetic vampire, feeding off the flesh of others.

Basilisk's whole body convulsed as he processed the new DNA. For a second Trojan thought that he was having a seizure. She reached out a hand to help, but then stopped—Basilisk's face was rippling like water, scars and wrinkles flattening out and shifting as they took on a new identity.

Bones crunched as they fortified themselves, and muscles rippled as he fed on the genetic characteristics of the tiny sample he had just absorbed. He felt stronger, rejuvenated. After a minute the convulsions stopped, and silence filled the *Nematode*.

"Man, are you okay?" asked Viral, who had been watching with professional interest.

Basilisk climbed out of the plush chair he sat in. His fingers crunched as he formed a fist.

"I feel great!" he exclaimed. "Now I feel I can take on the world!"

The others stared at him in surprise. Basilisk's completely blue eyes shone with youth and his face had taken on a new shape. It was still older and scarred from centuries of genetic tampering, but there was an unmistakable familiarity about him.

Viral frowned. "You know, now you look like that geek, the prisoner we had with the glasses."

* * *

Toby rubbed his tired eyes. The video images on-screen looped for the third time. They were surveillance cameras in Diablo Island Penitentiary, and what they showed was the beginning of a nightmare.

The prison had been badly damaged by the two previous escapes and there was no way it could resist a third assault. A gang of supervillains had teamed together to free their comrades held inside. Enforcers were stretched to a breaking point as they struggled to resist. The enemy forces were swelling with each prisoner they freed.

Mr. Grimm hadn't looked away from the screen on his desk. "The damage is incalculable. Decades of evil tyranny are unleashed on the world again."

"Shouldn't we be doing something about this?" asked Pete.

"We can't. If you try to deal with the escape at Diablo, that will leave the Foundation wide open. It's imperative that you protect the headquarters. You must travel to Mongolia immediately."

"Mongolia?" exclaimed Pete. "What's there? Apart from . . . um . . . "

"That's where the Foundation has relocated. Basilisk may try and paralyze the Hero satellite first, but—"

"You have your own satellite?" Pete blurted out.

"We have many things you don't know about. If he

The Beginning of a Nightmare

uses Worm and Viral to take the satellite, then it won't make any difference if we bring Hero.com online, as we will be unable to use it. The Foundation will still be defenseless."

"How can Basilisk reach a satellite? He doesn't have a spacecraft . . . does he?" asked Toby.

"Not as far as we know. But he's resourceful. I have no doubt he has already thought of a way to get his team into orbit and infect the satellite. That is why you should go straight to the Foundation."

The room fell silent. Mr. Grimm glanced at his watch as though he needed to be elsewhere. Lorna toyed with a small globe on Grimm's desk and rotated it around so she could see Mongolia perched above China. Then an unlikely connection raced through her mind, a casual comment she'd heard recently. "Yaks!"

Toby frowned. "What?"

"Yaks . . . that's what Mongolia has!"

"Big deal."

She looked at Mr. Grimm with wide eyes. "We have to hurry. We're not going to Mongolia! I think I know how Basilisk is going to bring down the satellite!"

Countdown to Extinction

Phase two was the one part of the plan that was out of Basilisk's control and relied on fate alone. It was also the one part of the plan that Worm didn't want to have anything to do with. Basilisk briefly thought it was an ideal opportunity to get rid of him, but remembered that he would need Worm's skills later.

The *Nematode* discreetly emerged from the ground a few miles from their target, and the four villains crouched low in the rocky terrain so they could get a clear view of the technological marvel in front of them. The space shuttle sat on its pad, vapors streaming from its multiple couplings as it was readied for launch. But this was no ordinary space shuttle.

The growing interest in space tourism meant that private investors had bought Russia's scrapped Buran space shuttle. Originally developed in the 1970s as a direct rival to the American shuttle, the Buran looked similar. It was marginally larger, as it sat on a powerful

Energia rocket. Only its four enormous boosters and tall fuel tank set it visibly apart from NASA's vehicle.

The entire rocket sat on the launch pad in Baikonur, Kazakhstan, adorned with sponsorship logos. It housed four astronauts, or cosmonauts, as the Russians preferred, and two billionaires who had spent millions of dollars on their four-day holiday aboard the International Space Station. The launch had already been delayed because a herd of yaks had invaded the fertile launch area.

"Are you sure about this?" Viral said in a low voice. He looked paler than ever, if that was physically possible.

Basilisk shot him a look. "Surely you're not frightened?"

"Of course not," Viral lied, and smiled weakly at Trojan. He had to try to impress the girl. "I just thought there could be *another* way we could do this."

"The satellite needs to be under our control and your powers only work in a one-hundred-foot radius. Even if we could get past the firewalls, there's no way you could transmit your virus to the satellite. But if you're close enough, Worm can get you directly into the system."

"Surely I can do that from the ground?" asked Worm. He was making no pretense of bravado. He was terrified.

"Impossible. The satellite has an internal network that, for safety reasons, is not accessible by computer from the ground. The only way Foundation technicians can reach it is to fly up there and access it wirelessly. Trojan will get us on board the shuttle. Once we're close, you will bypass the satellite's electronic systems and open it up for Viral to infect. And I need to be there to make sure you don't mess everything up! So *yes*, we all need to be there."

"Happy little team," quipped Trojan. She was excited about the journey ahead. It sure beat robbing museums and dusty bank vaults.

A siren whooped across the complex followed by a countdown in both Russian and English. "T-minus sixty seconds."

"This is it, Trojan. Get us inside—we're about to perform one of the most daring hijacks in history."

Inside the cockpit of the shuttle, the three crew members were strapped to their seats, flat on their backs, facing the clear blue sky above them. American commander John Mather, Russian pilot Irenus Markov, and British flight engineer Rebecca Syms went through the final checks before launch. Their mission specialist and two tourists sat in the payload bay section of the shuttle during takeoff.

"T-minus forty seconds," said the voice of Mission Control over their headsets.

"All systems go," Commander Mather reported,

unaware of the new additions that had quantum tunneled into their payload.

Trojan had misjudged their position—and the four villains fell several feet to land on the rear wall, which at the moment was the floor due to the craft's vertical position. The payload bay was filled with supplies for the International Space Station, and partitioned so that a passenger cabin at the front could accommodate tourists. Worm sprained his ankle when he landed and yelped in pain. Viral fell next to him. Only Trojan reached out and attached herself to the wall, demonstrating another of her powers, the ability to cling to sheer surfaces like a lizard.

"Wait here and prepare for launch by lying flat," Basilisk commanded Viral and Worm. He pointed to a computer terminal recessed in the wall next to them. "Worm, connect Viral into the system. Override Mission Control's remote access to the ship."

Basilisk then flew up to the bulkhead door and smashed the pressure hatch open with a single punch. Trojan quickly climbed after him.

The mission specialist looked around in alarm as Basilisk entered. She barked something in Russian. One of the two tourists pulled out his camera and took a picture, the flash creating spots in front of Basilisk's eyes.

"Trojan, deal with them!"

Basilisk powered through the cockpit door, yanking it

off its hinges. The door fell back down the entire length of the ship, where it smashed between Worm and Viral.

The tight harnesses prevented the crew from turning fully around as Basilisk levitated into the cockpit to collective gasps of amazement.

"T-minus thirty seconds," said the oblivious Mission Control. "Countdown handed to Buran. Godspeed, guys."

Commander Mather reacted instantly. "Abort! Abort! Mission Control—"

"Tough luck, Commander. Mission Control is out of the loop. You're taking us straight up."

Flight Engineer Rebecca Syms thumped the quick-release on her harness and lunged for Basilisk. She slugged him across the face, and Basilisk, caught off guard, stumbled into a control bank. The pilot and commander both moved to free themselves—but Basilisk snapped out with lightning speed and grabbed the woman around the throat.

"No! You move and she dies! I suggest you cooperate and we all get ready for launch."

"T-minus twenty seconds."

It was pure luck whose glitching powers enabled them to fly, and luck was with Toby and Pete. Once again Grimm reminded them that the powers could wear off or take on unwanted side effects at any moment, but they had insisted that they follow Lorna's hunch and head to Kazakhstan rather than Mongolia.

Mr. Grimm had canceled the stabilizing effect of the wristbands and after giving new ones to Lorna and Pete, had given them the last vial of artificial teleportation powers so they could jump to the launch site. The Foundation had been frantically trying to get through to the Kazakhstan mission control, unaware that Viral had infected and blocked all outside communications.

Now Toby and Pete were flying straight for the mighty Buran shuttle poised for launch on the pad.

"Wow! It's just like the real one!" said Pete in awe.

"It *is* a real one!"

"You know what I mean. Look! Basilisk!" shouted Pete as they neared. Sure enough, through the cockpit windows they could see Basilisk and Trojan lying flat against the bulkhead, in readiness for launch.

"T-minus sixteen," echoed the voice over the PA system. A water tower adjacent to the pad unleashed more than 250,000 gallons of water, which would absorb the sound of the boosters igniting.

Both heroes landed on the nose of the shuttle—using one of their stealth powers left over from Mexico, the ability to stick to walls. It was the same power Toby had experienced the first time they'd logged onto Hero.com. They peered through the window at stunned faces. The crew couldn't believe that two children had climbed up the shuttle seconds before launch—and Basilisk was brimming with fury.

"I just hope Lorna and Emily can stop the count-down in time," shouted Toby, "or this will get really complicated!"

Lorna, Emily, and Mr. Grimm had teleported directly into Mission Control. The technicians had panicked—and armed security raced into the room.

"Stop the launch!" Lorna bellowed.

The guards raised their guns and Emily pointed a hand at them—and hoped her erratic powers wouldn't harm the guards too much. Instead the metal guns jerked from their grip and flew toward her—as did many other metal items not bolted down. Emily was struck to the floor by a cascade of flying metal objects that buried her.

"Listen to the girl," said Mr. Grimm in his ever-calm tone. "There are hijackers aboard the shuttle."

The Mission Controller stared at him. He'd worked many years for NASA before taking on this private, and better paid, job. He'd seen many weird things in his time—although people teleporting into his Command Center was certainly high on the list. But his professional sense overruled any alarm he felt.

A technician called out. "We've lost contact with the

shuttle. It looks like we have a computer virus over-riding the system!"

"You've got to do something!" Lorna said desperately.

"T-minus ten."

A technician looked up. "The noise suppression system is activated!"

The Mission Controller shook his head as the automated countdown continued.

"She's going to launch—and there's not a thing we can do about it!"

Basilisk's eyes shone brightly—but both heroes ducked away from the cockpit windows before the petrification could affect them.

"Get out there and stop them!" he shouted at Trojan.

She reacted in surprise. "Me?"

"I can't have them ruining the plan! We've come too far!"

"I don't think it's stopping," Pete said with a tremor of apprehension as the entire spacecraft rumbled with pent-up power.

"T-minus eight—" The voice was drowned out as hydrogen igniters activated in each of the powerful engines.

"I don't think we thought this through," exclaimed Pete. "How are we going to stop it?"

"I don't know!"

"You're supposed to be our fearless leader!" yelled Pete.

"You can't stop us, boys," said Trojan as she appeared from thin air. She scuttled across the nose cone like a gecko.

Pete snarled. He remembered the experience of being imprisoned with Trojan. He lashed out and was happy to see an energy blast shoot over her head—exploding against the steel gantry supporting the shuttle.

Everybody's next move was cut short as the count-down reached six seconds and the main engines started. Stuck on the nose cone of the shuttle it sounded like the Big Bang, and they could feel their insides vibrate in a nauseating fashion.

"What do we do?" screamed Toby. But he couldn't hear his own words. He also didn't see Trojan throw her plasma disk at him. It slammed into Toby's chest with such force he rolled off the nose cone. . . .

And was only saved from falling as his hand attached him like a limpet to the side of the shuttle. He had trouble breathing and wondered if he'd broken a rib.

Then his whole world blew apart.

Water from the sound suppression system had hit

the flames from the main engines and sent colossal clouds of white steam around the base of the vehicle. Toby felt a wave of heat roll across his body. Then the launch pad swung away and the shuttle punched forward into the sky.

Inside, Basilisk, Worm, and Viral were thrown flat against the bulkheads. They felt a great weight on their chests as the g-force increased. Basilisk possessed a greater strength than most humans, so the acceleration was not as bad for him.

In the Command Center, Lorna and Emily watched the launch with a sinking feeling. The numerous video cameras around the site clearly showed Trojan and Pete crushed flat against the nose cone and Toby dangling from the side.

Pete was right over the nose cone as it cleared the tower. He unconsciously mustered superstrength from his random powers and the pain he felt from the g-force immediately subsided. He was now able to look up.

Trojan was not too far away, and it was only her adhesion power that prevented her from falling off. She gathered her strength and laboriously crawled toward Pete.

Toby felt as though his arms were popping from their sockets. He glanced down to see the ground spiraling as the shuttle rolled onto its back so that the giant rocket carrying them up was now *above* his head.

He secured his hands and feet. Like Pete, some inner reserve of power welled up and took the g-force pressure away, allowing him to scuttle back up the shuttle in time to see Trojan's plasma disk smash into Pete's face, almost dislodging his glasses.

Pete rolled uncontrollably off the nose cone—and managed to stick to the flat black underbelly of the shuttle—falling into the gap between the Energia rocket and the shuttle. He glanced down and realized that, had he slipped down the full length, the powerful rocket thrusters that were carrying them to the heavens would have vaporized him. And he was certain *none* of his superpowers would have saved him from that.

Toby unleashed a lightning bolt from his fingertips that bounced from the shuttle's heat tiles. Trojan threw herself aside, only just avoiding it.

The shuttle rolled again, and both she and Toby flailed for balance as they saw the ground move below them. Neither knew it, but they had just breached the sound barrier, and only their superhuman powers kept them attached to the side of the shuttle. The intense rush of wind made it impossible to talk, so Toby settled for another lightning blast—just as Trojan threw a plasma disk. The two projectiles collided in the air with a loud bang as they canceled one another out. Toby blinked because of the flash—and Trojan was gone. He assumed she must have been thrown off.

Countdown to Extinction

Toby frantically tried to think how they could bring the shuttle down without injuring the crew inside. It seemed like an impossible task. He didn't notice that Trojan had scuttled to the side of the fuselage so she could approach him unseen. She threw a punch.

Toby felt his jaw click and stars flashed before his eyes. He skidded down the side of the shuttle—and was alarmed to discover he had no grip left.

His adhesive ability was gone!

Trojan didn't think she had hit the boy that hard— but Toby slipped from the side of the shuttle and fell.

He caught the lip of the shuttle's delta wing. His enhanced strength was the only thing preventing him from plunging to a fiery death among the boosters. He was briefly aware that the sky was becoming darker above him and a rich blue beneath him. He knew they must be seconds away from both suffocation and being fried in the atmosphere.

Trojan dashed over to him and pulled one of Toby's hands free. Her grip was excruciating—but the pain was forgotten as he looked past her. She frowned and followed his gaze. Pete was crouched, inverted, on the booster rocket above them.

He grinned wickedly and made the funniest comment of his life—which was lost to the wind and roaring engines—before hurling an ice ball at Trojan. It hit her cape and bounced off, but it was strong enough to make her lose her balance. She dropped and found herself hanging from the opposite side of the delta wing from Toby.

Toby felt his grip weakening, but he knew if he could just hold on, his friend would come to his rescue. Then the entire shuttle vibrated and a series of explosions sounded.

The rocket booster had been jettisoned.

With Pete still clinging to it.

Toby watched Pete's face grow smaller as the booster peeled away, poised against the curving planet, falling back to earth.

His attention was torn back to the shuttle's nose as air friction caused it to glow. Then flames erupted across it and, seconds later, across the wing edge he was clinging to. He felt a stab of pain as the flames flickered across his hands. He wondered why the power that was keeping him alive at such oxygen-depleted altitude was not insulating him from the heat. The pain was so intense that he was forced to let go.

Toby fell.

He watched as Trojan slipped from the wing too and vanished beneath the folds of her cape, which disappeared into nothingness.

The roar of the wind deafened him, and his back took the brunt of the air pressure. He saw that the shuttle was now a flaming dart accelerating away, powered by its three orbital maneuvering system boosters on the rear.

Toby felt an odd sense of calm. He was so high that he would be falling for several minutes before he hit the earth. Their mission had failed.

He rolled onto his front; whatever shielding power allowed him to breathe and survive the g-forces was still active, as the air did not rip out his lungs as he fell. He kicked forward, intending to fly and find Pete before they landed.

Nothing happened.

He tried again, but there was no glimmer of him being able to control his descent. Now feeling panic for the very first time, Toby realized that his powers of flight had also abandoned him.

Pete was angry that they had failed to stop the shuttle— he had been calculating a plan just as the Energia rocket had detached and ruined everything. He watched the shuttle helplessly as he fell away from it, riding the booster toward the ground.

He had seen enough shuttle launches on TV to know that a parachute would be deployed to bring the booster, and himself, safely to earth. He only cursed his luck that Basilisk had slipped through his fingers.

Pete took in the rare view from such a high altitude.

It was only then that he noticed something else in the sky. Pete had to concentrate hard, but he was sure the dot was either Trojan or Toby. The shuttle had been traveling so fast that the figure must be miles away. Without pausing to think, Pete leaped from the booster and soared effortlessly through the air.

He willed himself to fly faster, aiming ahead of the falling figure to intercept it. He decided that if it was Trojan, he would just let her fall. His conscience reminded him that the fall would splatter her. But before he could dwell on any more macabre thoughts, he identified the figure as Toby and wondered why he wasn't flying.

Pete matched pace with Toby, who looked like a parachutist.

"Great view, huh?" It was lame, but it was all Pete could think of to avoid talking about their recent defeat.

"Fantastic!" Toby screamed. "Wish I had a camera with me." He stared at Pete, who didn't seem to get the danger he was in. Toby prompted him. "Well?"

"What?"

"Aren't you going to ask me why I'm free-falling?"

"Quickest way down?"

Toby bit back a curse. Now wouldn't be the best time for the friends to fight. "No, Pete. I've lost my powers. I can't fly."

"Ah . . . that's a big problem."

Countdown to Extinction

Toby felt like punching Pete, but restrained himself. "So, a little help? That would be . . . wonderful."

The expression on his friend's face reminded Pete that this was a potentially fatal situation. The ground was beginning to form real definition, with roads and railway tracks becoming visible. Luckily they could still see the vapor trail left by the Buran shuttle, leading to Mission Control.

Pete swooped under Toby, as if he were about to offer him a piggyback ride.

"Grab my shoulders and hold on."

Pete felt Toby grip his shoulders so hard that just a little more pressure would have broken a bone. He banked away, and hoped that Toby's added weight wouldn't plunge them both to their deaths.

With no help from the crew, the Buran's computer system put the ship into orbit and Basilisk was finally free to float next to the commander.

"If you do as I say, then I have no problem with you all living out the rest of your lives. Do you understand?"

Commander Mather glanced behind him at his passengers in the payload bay. They had been slumped in their seats since Trojan had dealt with them, but the small monitors that tracked their heart and pulse rates bleeped rhythmically, indicating that they were alive. The rest of his crew met his glance and gave curt nods.

"Very well," said the commander. "If it gets you off my ship, what do you want?"

Basilisk reached over to a computer system and typed in a coordinate. "You will bring the shuttle around on this trajectory so that we can intercept a satellite."

"Then what? You gonna spacewalk over to it?"

"There will be no need for such risks, Commander. Get us close enough so we can communicate directly through the shuttle's wireless network. Then you'll turn us around, and land right back on the ground. All in one piece. *All* of us alive."

"That's it?" said the commander, perplexed. "You could have done that from the ground."

"No we couldn't. This is a very *special* satellite." Basilisk clapped his hands, making a sound like bricks clinking. "Come on! Time is of the essence."

Pete opened his eyes and saw nothing but dust. Somewhere in the distance he could hear ambulance sirens. He blinked and looked around. He was lying at the end of a thousand-foot trench that he'd just gouged in the earth.

It had turned out that Toby's additional weight did make them lose altitude at a much faster rate than Pete was comfortable with. He had fought hard to approach the ground at a gentle angle, but Toby had caused them to come in fast.

They overshot the launch complex at Baikonur and soared out into the surrounding rocky hills. At the very last moment, Toby had attempted to create a protective shield around them, but he only managed half a sphere around their feet. Pete had been able to twist around so they were descending feetfirst.

The shield acted like a snowboard as they hit the hillside at almost one hundred miles per hour. It gouged the earth, spitting rocks and debris in their wake. In the final few moments, the shield wavered as the powers glitched—turning the shield into ice that shattered underfoot. They tumbled the last couple of feet, picking up cuts and scratches. Pete was amazed that his glasses had survived.

Toby sat up next to him, dust turning his hair gray. He coughed. "Well, I won't be forgetting that experience any time soon!"

Both boys then broke into laughter, so hard that tears filled their eyes. By the time the base's four-wheel-drive ambulances had traversed the hills, the paramedics were surprised to find two crying, giggling boys. Lorna and Emily were in the back of one of the ambulances. Their concerned expressions immediately changed to ones of annoyance.

"You let them get away!" Lorna fumed.

Toby shook his head, still giggling. "It's not like we didn't try, Lorn."

Lorna crossed her arms and her lips formed a pout. "Well, now Mr. Grimm is insisting we head straight to Mongolia. You have no time to clean up."

Both boys stared at each other for the first time—the dust clung to them so it looked as if they'd both been dipped in flour. They pointed at one another and burst into laughter again.

Lorna shook her head irritably. *Boys*, she thought.

It took Commander Mather only a few hours to bring the Buran into a new orbit, and soon their instruments picked up the satellite gently revolving in its geosynchronous orbit; sunlight glistened off its golden heat shields, black solar panels, and the Hero Foundation's logo on its side.

Basilisk had left no calculation to chance, and ordered Commander Mather to bring the shuttle within thirty feet of the satellite. This close they could see it was the size of a van and it looked relatively new. Basilisk remotely accessed the satellite using the shuttle's systems; a function used by authorized crews to wirelessly and directly access satellites. He immediately hit the satellite's own firewall and handed the console over to Worm.

Countdown to Extinction

Worm was pleased to have a distraction. Floating in zero-g had made him throw up, and now the back of the payload bay was a no-go area because of the sea of floating awfulness.

He touched the computer screen and allowed the electrons forming his fingers to zip into the system. Once inside it was a simple case of blindly probing the software until he was allowed through into the satellite's operating system. He gritted his teeth at the pain.

When he closed his eyes, Worm could see the flow of data, like tiny cars flying through aerial roadways as they transferred data to and from ground stations. Basilisk had tried to explain he was seeing a rare and wonderful thing called "cyberspace"—an electronic realm few people would ever actually see.

Once Worm was done, he brought the satellite's firewall down, leaving it wide open to attack. Now it was Viral's turn. He had to create a virus that would not affect the shuttle's own systems, but would hitch a ride on the data pathway Worm had just opened and override the satellite, holding it in limbo until either he or Basilisk chose to bring it back online.

The virus had taken some planning and concentration to create. Viral had always known he could interact with protein threads and DNA strands within nature, enabling him to create the most devastating viruses ever seen on the planet. It was only at the end of his teens that he realized that, with a bit of effort, he could manipulate electrons to form malignant computer viruses. His very first one had successfully crashed the world's stock market computers, sending global economies tumbling. The only drawback he had with his powers was that the viruses—whether physical or digital—were so destructive that they only had a life span of a few minutes before they tore themselves apart.

"Hurry!" grunted Worm. The pain in his fingers was becoming unbearable and he thought he was going to pass out.

"Okay, first code's going in." Viral transferred his electronic bug with nothing more visible than a spark between his fingers and the screen.

Basilisk stared at the screen. The first part of the virus would ping the Foundation servers. The answer he got back would contain the location of the Foundation Headquarters—secret information that would be stored on the satellite, inaccessible from the ground.

Coordinates flashed up on the shuttle's screen. Basilisk laughed out loud.

"We have it! Well done!"

Viral grinned, revealing his stained teeth. "Easy. Now I'll insert the malware code to bring down their physical defenses."

The villains were so wrapped up in the operation

that they didn't notice Commander Mather give a small gesture to his crew.

Viral was conjuring one last strand of contamination when the pilot unclipped a small metal medical kit. He brought it around with such force on the back of Viral's head that he was struck instantly unconscious and spun head over heels to the back of the payload bay, splashing into the floating vomit left by Worm.

Worm opened his mouth to speak but felt a strap loop around his fat neck and tighten to choke him. Rebecca Syms was behind him, her knee in the small of his back and screaming with exertion as she throttled the villain. With his concentration lost, the communications with the satellite were severed, with only part of Viral's code having seeped through.

Basilisk spun around and glared at Commander Mather, who threw a punch straight at him, but it didn't even faze the villain.

"You've made a terrible mistake, Commander."

Commander Mather didn't listen—he braced himself against the control panel and used both feet to boot Basilisk in the chest. On earth, Basilisk's immense strength would render him immovable by any normal human. But the weightlessness robbed him of his advantage. Basilisk shot into the payload bay like a bullet. Rebecca Syms followed suit with Worm, tossing him into Basilisk.

The zero-g environment had given the normal humans an edge over the supervillains. Irenus Markov hit a button, and emergency decompression doors closed across the payload. The Russian's hand hovered over a button marked "airlock," but Commander Mather stopped him.

"Markov, no! You'll jettison the passengers if you open the airlock. I need you to prepare for reentry *now*!"

The crew took their seats without question.

Basilisk was furious, but he had to contain his outrage, as he risked blowing a hole in the side of the shuttle if he blasted the partition. That would depressurize the entire ship, suck the oxygen into space and kill them all. The lack of gravity meant they could not detect if the shuttle was moving, but a slight tremor through the fuselage indicated the boosters had ignited.

Viral was still unconscious as Worm and Basilisk argued over strategies for breaking through the bulkhead door. Everything seemed too risky; this was one situation where their superpowers proved completely useless. At least they had the Foundation's location, and some of the code had been transferred into the satellite, hopefully damaging it enough to stay off-line.

For a few hours nothing seemed to happen, except

the thrusters continued to fire on and off. Basilisk correctly assumed that the shuttle was positioning for re-entry.

Then the Buran started to shimmy violently and the villains could feel the gentle pull of gravity tug at them. Viral regained consciousness just as gravity took hold and he slammed to the floor on his back.

"What's happening?" he asked groggily.

"We're heading back to Earth. Hold on tight!"

Hero.com

It was the most blissful, wonderful experience Toby could remember. And then Pete had woken him up from the deep slumber. Toby forced an eye open and was greeted by harsh sunlight. He yawned and wished that he could roll over in a warm bed and sleep for an entire day.

"Where are we?"

"You've slept all night. We're here."

Immediately after they had been picked up in Kazakhstan, Mr. Grimm had declared that they were heading straight to Mongolia, the current location of Hero Foundation headquarters, to face Basilisk in the final showdown.

Toby was excited at the prospect. He felt as though he was entering a mystic world where all his questions about Hero.com would finally be answered. The FAQ guide on the site had been lacking, and he guessed that not many people bothered asking questions.

Midway through the flight, Mr. Grimm had announced that Basilisk had succeeded in taking the

Foundation's satellite off-line. The technicians who had been working night and day to restore Hero.com had toiled for nothing.

There would be no cavalry arriving to help now.

It was up to them.

The only powers left were the ones they had over-dosed on the day Basilisk had inserted his virus into Hero.com. And they wouldn't last very long either.

Toby was lost in his thoughts, only becoming aware several minutes later that he had been staring at Emily, who was trying to sleep. He looked away guiltily, only to find that Pete was looking straight at him with a stony expression.

Toby tried to break the atmosphere with a smile. "Can't sleep, man?" Pete shook his head, but didn't say anything. "Look, about what you said earlier, us not being a team . . . "

"We're a lousy team and you know it."

"What? We're great, we work well together—"

"Maybe in your mind we do. You don't let us go on the Web site when we want to. You were against a team name, costumes, *everything* that I suggested." The bitterness in his voice was unmistakable.

"That's not true!" protested Toby, although he could see Pete's point all too clearly. "Besides, we need a leader to keep the group—"

"Nobody voted you leader. You know what unelected

leaders are called? Dictators. We learned that in class last week, if you remember."

Toby was at a loss for words. His best friend was attacking him, and worse, he knew his best friend was right.

"I'll be better off on my own. Like when you all left me with Basilisk."

Toby closed his eyes. He knew this was the core of the problem. "Pete, honestly we had no idea . . . we were stupid to leave you alone."

Pete's voice rose, causing Emily to stir in her sleep. "Yeah, you were! But I should thank you. That's when I learned that I have to look out for myself and not count on my friends or my *family*!" He spat the last word out, and a new wave of guilt passed over Toby. With all that had happened, they'd had no time to talk about Pete's parents' divorce. Toby opened his mouth to reply, but Pete had already turned his back on him, pretending to sleep.

Toby sighed. It wasn't so much the breakup of his superteam that bothered him; it was the fact that his friends were all changing, becoming more distant. Worse still, he suspected it was his own fault. While he thought he was protecting his friends, he was in fact causing harm.

He thought back to Mr. Grimm's words about the world needing balance. They were starting to make sense.

When Pete finally woke him up, Toby found they

had landed on an airstrip in the middle of nowhere. In fact, *airstrip* was too kind a word. It was just a flat piece of rock-strewn desert. Mountains rippled in the heat haze to the south.

"We're here," said Mr. Grimm.

"Where is *here* exactly?" Toby asked.

Mr. Grimm walked with them to a Toyota Land Cruiser.

"Climb in. We don't have much time. '*Here*' is the Gobi desert in Mongolia."

The air-conditioned interior of the 4x4 was a relief after the short sweltering steps they had taken. Before the car doors had even shut, the Gulfstream jet had taxied around and was accelerating for takeoff.

"Don't believe in waiting, do they?" Pete mumbled.

"Why wait in such an inhospitable place? Believe it or not, it's the winter here at the moment," said Mr. Grimm as they jounced across the landscape. His expression still hadn't changed, nor had he reacted to the heat outside or the frigid air-conditioning inside the vehicle. "It's warmer than usual, but at night, temperatures have been plummeting to about minus thirty degrees."

Toby and Pete exchanged knowledgeable looks. They had survived in the snowy plains of Antarctica. The Gobi desert was a piece of cake by comparison.

"Why is the Hero Foundation headquarters here?" asked Emily staring out at the bleak landscape.

"It's not normally here," Mr. Grimm said cryptically. "But due to recent events, this was the best place to hide it. Isolated, remote, and unlikely to be stumbled upon by civilians during a time of clandestine war."

Everybody frowned, but Lorna was the first to ask. "What do you mean, war? Who's at war?"

"We are, against the villains overthrowing society. Things are now completely out of control."

Toby shook his head. Despite their adventures so far on Diablo Island, in the Mexican jungle, and fighting for their lives on a space shuttle, they had not paid much attention to the rest of the world. It was changing. Pete summed it up eloquently.

"Well, darn. We'd better get a move on then!"

Mr. Grimm pointed ahead. "It seems we've arrived."

The Buran shuttle shook with fury as it blistered through the atmosphere. Searing flames caused by air friction tore across the black heat tiles on the underside of the craft.

Inside, the g-force pinned everybody to the wall. Everybody except Basilisk, who was hovering in the center of the payload bay.

"We're entering the atmosphere," he snarled. "At least we'll have air to breathe!"

Before the others could object, Basilisk hurled an energy blast at the cockpit door, ripping a hole clean through it. He flew inside, oblivious to the g-force. The three crew members were pinned to their seats, only their eyes swiveled toward the villain. They had been lulled into a false sense of security by the villains' lack of effort at reentering the cockpit. And now, at a critical stage, one had regained his strength.

Irenus Markov was piloting the craft with an airplane-style control stick. He jerked it to one side. The shuttle lurched to port and Basilisk crashed his head against the overhead instrument panel. The supervillain responded by yanking Markov from his seat with such force that his restraining harness snapped.

"No!" bellowed Commander Mather. "You'll kill us all!"

Basilisk's petrifying gaze bored into the Russian. Markov screamed and fought to escape, but within seconds his movements failed as his skin turned to stone. Basilisk applied pressure—and the man's petrified body crumpled to dust. The remaining crew stared at Basilisk with open mouths.

"Now land us where I tell you!" shouted Basilisk.

"We can't," said Mather in a small voice. "You just killed the *pilot*!"

Basilisk hesitated. He'd let rage control him and now he'd killed the wrong guy. He stabbed a finger at Commander Mather.

"You can fly this. Land at these coordinates." Basilisk spun easily through the air and typed on a computer terminal. Seconds later a map of the world appeared, complete with flight trajectories to enable them to land where he had indicated.

With little choice, Mather took control of the aircraft. The g-force had lessened and he had to fight to keep the shuttle's nose above the horizon. It had to glide to earth without the aid of engines to control it.

Basilisk climbed into the vacant pilot's seat and watched as the earth formed around him. The commander angled the shuttle around, matching the computer's trajectory perfectly.

"Good. I should warn you. There is no runway to land on."

The commander shot him a look of hatred. "Then you'll still kill us all. The ship is not designed for off-roading!"

"That is not my problem."

Commander Mather stared at the freak, then calmly said something in Russian to Rebecca Syms. Basilisk assumed it was all part of the sequence, since they had been taking off and landing in Kazakhstan. He did not notice Mather or Syms tightening their harnesses. Seconds later Mather reached under his seat and yanked a handle.

Basilisk had no idea the single word Mather had spoken translated as *eject*.

The commander stared at Basilisk. "Now it *is* your problem."

His seat ejected through the roof with a bang. Syms followed seconds later—followed by three more explosions from the payload bay as the unconscious mission specialist and both tourists were also ejected.

The ejector seats had been under the sole control of the commander and he was able to eject the crew and passengers safely. The ejector seats had parachutes and tracking beacons built in, so the unconscious trio would land safely and be found quickly.

Basilisk stared at the controls in disbelief. He had only ever flown his own invention, the SkyKar, and that had been destroyed weeks ago. He briefly considered simply flying to safety, but then remembered Worm and Viral couldn't fly—and he still needed them for the final phase. If they died now it would have all been for nothing.

"You two! Get on the flight deck now!"

He pushed forward on the stick to level the aircraft with the horizon—but the altimeter seemed to descend even more quickly. Viral and Worm entered the cockpit at a run.

"What happened?"

"The crew ejected and left us to die," Basilisk said bitterly. It was never pleasant to be on the blunt end of selfishness.

Viral propped himself against the engineer's console—with the seats gone he could do little else. He stared at the ground, which seemed to be filling up too much of the view outside.

"Can you fly?"

Basilisk hesitated. "Personally: yes. If you mean an aircraft: no."

Worm indicated that he wanted Basilisk's seat. "Let me try."

"You?" Basilisk exclaimed, swapping places with the little man.

"You've angled the nose too much and put us in a dive. It has to be just above the horizon, like this."

Worm pulled back on the stick—too hard. The shuttle lifted almost vertically up and lost so much speed that engine stall warnings bleeped across the cockpit.

"Push back!" screamed Viral as he was thrown against the wall.

Worm pushed forward and the shuttle's nose dropped below the horizon—and suddenly they were plummeting to the ground. He pulled back and managed to level out. Basilisk had gripped the instrument panel so hard his superstrong fingers had left dents in it.

"The controls are more sensitive than when I last flew," said Worm by way of explanation.

"When did you last fly?" asked Basilisk, unsure if he wanted to hear the answer.

"It was a Sopwith Camel biplane back in—"

"The First World War?"

Viral gripped the console. "Oh my God! You learned to fly *just after* they invented the airplane!"

Vital seconds passed and nobody dared speak. Basilisk looked at the computer display and noticed they had drifted from their trajectory. He tapped the screen.

"This red line is us. Keep it matched with the blue line. *Carefully!*"

Worm gently realigned the aircraft. Basilisk had to admit he was picking up basic flying pretty well.

"We should be decelerating," said Worm. "Where are the flaps?"

They hunted around the controls—most of which were labeled in Russian, with a few makeshift paper labels handwritten in English—hardly high tech. None of them said *flaps*. Worm was so wrapped up in squinting at the labels that he didn't notice the mountain peaks rise up in front of them.

Viral pointed a finger, but couldn't speak. Now he knew what terror felt like and swore to himself that he'd abandon his villainous ways if only he got out of this alive. Worm looked up, just in time.

WHOOSH! The Buran rolled onto its side and shot through the twin peaks at such a speed that the displaced air caused avalanches on both mountains.

He leveled out again, but the altimeter was revolving like a crazy clock. Ahead the air was arid and dry. Basilisk glanced at the computer screen and was surprised to see that Worm had kept them pretty much on course. The landing zone was just ahead—but was rapidly becoming a crash zone.

"We need to lose speed quickly!" shouted Basilisk. "The landing zone isn't far."

Viral spotted a control on the engineer's console, labeled with a handwritten note. "Got it! It says parachute!"

Basilisk spun around. "Don't—!"

Too late. Virus mashed the button. He didn't know that the parachute is deployed only once the shuttle is safely on the runway to slow it down.

An explosive charge at the rear of the shuttle blew a panel away and the parachute unfolded. Since the shuttle was still airborne, the effect was as though the spacecraft had reached the end of a tether and was flipped backward.

The Buran corkscrewed through the air as the parachute expanded and became twisted because of the aircraft's motions. Dozens of alarms sounded in the cockpit—Viral was thrown around as if he were trapped in a washing machine. Basilisk remained hovering, so the rotating room did not affect him, and luckily Worm had *just* strapped himself into the pilot's chair.

The aircraft completed four barrel rolls as the rear undercarriage scuffed the desert floor, and almost disintegrated.

Basilisk yelled: "The landing gear!" But it was too late to act.

The rest of the Buran shuttle belly flopped onto the desert floor. Boulders and rocks ground away the heat shield and shattered both wings as the aircraft slid for half a mile. It soared off several ridges—briefly becoming airborne—then smashed back to earth.

The Buran raced toward a huge finger of rock poking from the parched earth. The rock struck amidships and ripped the billion-dollar vehicle in half. Both halves spun away. The tail section rolled end-over-end, the engines ripping themselves apart. The cockpit fared better and crunched to a halt in the gully of a dry riverbed, upside down.

Dust filled the air, and for a long time nothing stirred.

Then a stone hand punched through the twisted fuselage, and Basilisk extracted himself from the wreck, his scars and cuts regenerating quickly. He could barely see his hand in front of his face because of the dust, and dropped to his knees, coughing.

He was alive. But he had no idea if the others were. The thought of failure struck him hard.

* * *

"Wow!"

It was the only word Pete could think of to describe the Hero Foundation headquarters.

They had seen what looked like a small city caught in a heat haze. It could have easily been a mirage. But as they got closer the young heroes saw that the haze was a huge wall of fire.

"Not the kind of firewall I was expecting," said Emily. Pete laughed but the other two either didn't get it, or were too amazed to say anything.

"It keeps people out," said Mr. Grimm.

The entire city was floating just above the desert floor.

"It flies?" asked Toby in amazement.

"Of course. How did you think it moved around?"

They approached a ramp extending down from the flames. As the Land Cruiser ascended, the flames pulled apart like a curtain, granting them access.

They all felt the heat as they passed through the wall, which rumbled like thunder. As soon as they were through, the headquarters presented itself.

It looked like a huge industrial processing plant for oil or gasoline, built on a giant circular platform. Gray steel structures and towers held a complex network of pipes that ran between hundreds of cylindrical glass tanks, each the size of a house and containing a variety of colorful thick liquids. Pipes and valves were connected to the tanks in a complex arrangement. The tanks themselves were displayed around the circular hub that consisted of several sleek tower blocks like a futuristic city. Transmitter towers and satellite dishes covered the buildings and a huge marble Hero Foundation logo was prominently displayed.

The scale of it all was mind-blowing. It was the size of a small town, crisscrossed with maintenance roads.

"We're approaching the hub," Mr. Grimm narrated, sounding like a travel agent, "where we have the research and development labs, strategy planning rooms, world-wide communications center, sleeping quarters, a restaurant, a gym, a sauna, and an excellent heated swimming pool with a wave machine."

"Those tanks hold the superpowers?" asked Lorna.

"Raw superpowers, donated by Primes across the world and throughout the ages, and some now replicated artificially. All so that you can have the privilege of being a superhero."

Lorna blinked. "Can artificial powers be bad for you?" She was constantly berating her mother for buying food with artificial preservatives in it.

"Well, they keep getting us in life-threatening situations," joked Toby, who was thoroughly enjoying the trip. For him it was better than a visit to a chocolate factory.

"Do not concern yourself, there are no proven health risks."

That didn't reassure Lorna. "Are they chemicals?"

"The best way to describe them is that they are a combination of energy plasma and cytoplasm cultures." He saw the blank expression on Lorna's face. "Living energy, in layman's terms."

"Cool," said Pete.

"I can't see any other people," said Toby.

"The entire station is controlled automatically and manned by a skeleton staff. Everybody else has been evacuated for safety reasons, and the Primes who chose to live here have left."

Mr. Grimm pulled up in a circular atrium. He gestured for the four of them to enter the posh marble lobby.

"Aren't you coming with us?" said Emily.

"I will be joining you later. But the, uh, boss would like to meet you."

Toby felt a thrill of excitement. "The boss? You mean Commander Courage?"

Mr. Grimm didn't reply. He pulled away and they walked toward the entrance. Lorna caught Emily's arm and pointed across the platform.

"Look!"

A soft white fog appeared around the perimeter. They looked up to see clouds rapidly approaching them—then suddenly billow around them.

"We must be ascending really fast," said Pete. "But I can't feel the movement."

The clouds suddenly parted, revealing a chilly clear blue sky all around them.

"Come on," said Toby. "Let's not keep the boss waiting."

Lorna and Pete exchanged a glance, an old argument welling up in their minds. *Boss* implied they were working for somebody, and Lorna and Pete both agreed that if that was the case then they should be getting paid for putting their lives on the line.

Since Lorna had started dating, she also felt a little more mature and was beginning to feel that Toby's and Emily's notions of risking their lives for the greater good were idealistic—not realistic.

Maybe it's time for change? she thought as they stepped through the revolving doors and into the marble lobby.

The lobby was huge. A Hero Foundation logo stood proudly in the center of the room, a fountain bubbling around it. It looked like a high-class hotel.

"Ah! Here at last!" said a man stepping from the shadows. "About time, too."

The man chuckled, but Lorna felt annoyed that he was reprimanding them. Toby was feeling the opposite. He was shaking with nervous excitement.

"Allow me to introduce myself. I'm the founder of the Higher Energy Research Organization—and the reason you are here. My name is Eric Kirby, but I once went by the name Commander Courage."

A Traitor's Revenge

"He's alive, barely," said Trojan as she felt Viral's pulse. Even though the man physically repulsed her, they had been getting along well. She would even consider him a friend, which was a rare gift in the world of villainy.

They sat in the shade offered by the smashed shuttle cockpit, and Basilisk weighed their options. Immediately after crashing, he had discovered both Worm and Viral were unconscious. Worm recovered quickly, but Viral had been crushed by the engineering console and was bleeding freely.

Luckily Trojan had used her initiative to track the shuttle and had quantum-tunneled to them the moment it crash-landed. She had been on hand to give Viral basic first aid, something neither of the other villains knew how to do. She just hoped that she wasn't going to catch anything from him.

"This is folly!" said Worm for the second time. "We risk our lives for what? A failed plan!"

Basilisk growled. "We must assume that enough of the virus hit the satellite network."

A Traitor's Revenge

"We are crawling in the dirt like animals, Basilisk. My mind was elsewhere when I decided to listen to your schemes! I should take you in to the Council of Evil, claim the reward, and be done with it!"

Basilisk's eyes flared. He still needed Worm once they were inside the Foundation headquarters so he could hack into the computer network. But if Viral died, then so did Worm's usefulness.

"I'm surprised you feel that way, especially since you're this close to killing Commander Courage."

Worm's eyes brightened at the thought of it.

Trojan suddenly spoke up. "I have an idea. Viral doesn't possess any healing factor. But he could download one from Villain.net."

Basilisk shook his head. "Viral is a Prime. And if a Prime downloads from the V-net system it will cause feedback loops and all kinds of chaos. *Trust me* on that."

"But it's the only way to save him."

Basilisk thought hard. The implications of connecting Viral to Villain.net posed the small risk that he would accidentally contaminate the network and bring that down too. It would also alert the Council of Evil to his whereabouts, since they would be closely monitoring their own systems after what Basilisk had achieved with Hero.com.

But it was a risk he was willing to take.

"You're right," he said, taking a small cell phone from

his belt. He thumbed through the menus and was connected to Villain.net, where he scrolled through the jumble of icons. He knew which one was regeneration: it had been one of *his* power contributions to Villain.net's cache of superpowers. He chose the option and turned the screen toward Viral. A small thin silver finger leaped out and tapped Viral on the head.

Viral instantly started to convulse, as if he'd been electrocuted, and his bloodshot eyes opened as he screamed. His bones cracked as they knitted together in seconds—his entire chest pushed back into shape with a crunch. Cuts healed and he suddenly sat upright.

"Wow! That felt great. What did you do to me?"

Trojan smiled. "Just a little pick-me-up."

Relief flooded Basilisk's face, although it was hidden from the others in the dark recesses of his hood.

"Excellent. And now, team, to battle and *victory*."

Toby was a bit disappointed. Commander Courage, or Eric as he now preferred, was an old man. Though his wrinkled face beamed pleasantly at them, and he sported a trimmed white mustache that complemented his pure white hair. He walked with a cane but seemed nimble enough.

Eric had led them into an elevator that had taken them to a spacious circular boardroom. A round table was in the center, monitors in front of each seat. A holographic globe spun at the center of the table, problem spots highlighted in red—and right now that was most of the planet.

The two halves of the room offered panoramic curved viewing windows across the grounds, ending in the flaming firewalls.

Eric pointed to the seats. "This is where the greatest superheroes who have ever lived sit to discuss how best to use their gifts for the greater good."

Pete spoke up first. "And your first thoughts were to get kids to pay for powers, then risk their lives to do your dirty work?"

Toby and Eric both looked at him in surprise.

"No, Pete. The plan was to give *anybody*—young or old—the opportunity to be a hero. If you are successful then we award Heroism points and the powers are free. If you fail, then you have to pay." The smile reappeared. "Think of it as a *motivation* to succeed. Plus, all this doesn't pay for itself, you know."

"Wouldn't it be better if *you* paid us?"

Eric shook his head. "Then your actions would be financially motivated. Guided by greed."

Pete looked out of the window and nodded. Toby was at his side, whispering.

"What's wrong with you?"

Pete made no attempt at hiding his anger. "It's obvious,

isn't it? Money's not good for us, but it's okay to pay *them* for the powers! They're just like any other big business—greedy and manipulative!"

Eric shook his head. "I assure you—"

"My parents are splitting up because we're broke. My house got destroyed and there's no way we can afford a new one, and yet I'm out here fighting for the so-called heroes! And what do I get out of it? *Nothing!* Are all the other great heroes who sat at this table worried about their parents? Wondering whether they have enough money to buy even the groceries? I bet they don't. I bet they're all rich!"

Emily gently laid a hand on his arm, and Pete magically calmed down. "Pete, we know it's not right. But this isn't the time. We're all fighting for the same side."

"I feel that Mr. Kendall sees an old man, and thinks I'm asking him to be the free help."

"That's right!" snapped Pete.

Toby's cheeks flushed with embarrassment at his friend's outburst. "He's just got a lot on his mind right now." He shot Pete a look that he hoped would silence him.

"Valiantly supporting your friends is an honorable trait. But I understand, I really do. Primes are a dying breed. There are fewer of us born each year when once there were many. You know, the legends from Greek mythology to Hollywood heroes—those people were Primes.

"We created the Hero Foundation to harvest Prime powers. We discovered a way to make powers tangible, and created a system to deliver them to people with no gifts at all. With most of us being too old to fight, we were forced into retirement, but we weren't going to go without a battle." He looked suddenly melancholy. "Alas, even superheroes age. Although not all of us at the same rate. I'm a hundred and three, but don't look a day over sixty-five. Least I like to think so.

"Rather than sell superpowers in a shop so that everyone could pick and choose . . . and ultimately cause mayhem, we decided to create an online Web site that would randomly select applicants, such as yourselves. Of course, complex algorithms monitored the kinds of people we looked for. Your Web searches were monitored and analyzed. Intellectual searches were flagged as being done by potentially good candidates, but if you were looking for trash or information on guns, for example, then you probably were not a suitable candidate."

"So we were chosen at random?" Toby said in surprise. He had been hoping for something that spoke of destiny.

Eric smiled enigmatically. "More or less."

Emily was about to argue that "random" did not mean "more or less," but Eric continued.

"But you do possess qualities that separate the real heroes from villains, regardless of powers or abilities."

"What are they?" asked Pete, curious.

"A developed sense of compassion and reasoning. The two most powerful attributes a person can have."

Pete pulled a face and shook his head. No way was that better than flying or shooting laser blasts.

Eric smiled. "You may not believe me, but because of the lack of those two attributes, we were betrayed by some heroes who broke away and formed the Council of Evil—"

"Heroes are running *that*?" Lorna exclaimed in surprise.

"*Ex*-heroes. From that point we knew it was dangerous to fully trust our own ranks. The traitors took the blueprints for Hero.com and the Council of Evil created Villain.net in direct opposition. But it wasn't as good as the original."

Pete let out a low whistle. "So heroes do become villains. Interesting."

Eric stared into space as though recalling something. "It can happen with the best of friends." He gave Toby a curious glance. "But that is something you wouldn't yet know."

What's that supposed to mean? thought Toby. He wondered if the old man was going senile.

* * *

A Traitor's Revenge

Having left the heroes with Commander Courage, Mr. Grimm drove the Land Cruiser to a building on the edge of the complex. Poised against the raging firewall was a squat bunker bedecked with satellite dishes. This was the main communication relay hub, and Commander Courage had asked him to discover what damage had been caused by Viral's incursion.

Inside sat a technician named Johnston who was busy studying streams of code on the screens. Mr. Grimm looked around.

"Have the rest of the support staff been evacuated?"

Johnston didn't look up. "Been relocated to the elemental subbases as a contingency in case we fail here."

"And is that likely to happen?"

Johnston tapped the code on the screen. "The satellite's off-line, but it hasn't been destroyed. This is one doozy of a bug. It has put the network to sleep for the next four hours or so, then the whole thing'll be back online as good as new. Just need to get this place pumping out the powers and we're back in business."

Mr. Grimm frowned. "Why would they attack the satellite, but not destroy it?"

"At a guess, they have no intention of destroying the Web site, just taking it over."

"To use against the Council, no doubt," mused Mr. Grimm.

Johnston looked at Mr. Grimm for the first time. "You think so?"

"Can you delay the system from coming back online?"

"Delay it? Why would I want to do that? We need the network on ASAP."

"Basilisk and his team are almost here. I want to make sure that if they do seize control of this facility, then they won't simply be waiting for the system to come back online."

"Sure. I'll get on it. But there's so much other stuff in here that I can't figure out . . . "

"I'm sure you will." Mr. Grimm spun on his heels and exited. He had heard all he needed to. He left the building and straightened his tie.

It was useful information to pass on to the Council of Evil. He had long traded secrets to the Council in return for obscene amounts of money, and occasionally fed the Hero Foundation information too. He was a double agent, paid by the good guys to protect their interests and by the bad guys for information on the Foundation. He revealed nothing too problematic that would bring about the fall of either organization, such as the locations of their headquarters and substations, but just enough to maintain a healthy competitive balance between the two sides, and keep himself earning a living.

The Council had asked him to assist Basilisk's final

assault, which he had no intention of doing. Even less, now that he'd uncovered Basilisk's true intentions. All Mr. Grimm now had to do was get out of the conflict zone.

A dull *whump* reverberated across the complex. Mr. Grimm's hand was on the door of the Land Cruiser when he looked up. The firewall had gone out—leaving a clear view of nothing but sky beyond. An intruder alarm immediately sounded across the complex.

Mr. Grimm felt a tingle of panic as he realized that the virus Basilisk had inserted into the satellite system had just lowered the shield, leaving the Foundation wide open to attack before he could leave.

Four figures materialized on the deck, striding out of the expansive folds of Trojan's cape. Before Mr. Grimm could open the car door, an energy blast slammed into the vehicle and knocked it over—leaving him holding nothing but a broken door handle.

"You will not be needing that, Grimm," shouted Basilisk. "This place is mine now."

"Basilisk, an unexpected pleasure—," began Mr. Grimm in passive tones.

"Shut up! I never liked your double-dealings when I was with the Council. And I certainly have no need for you now."

Johnston appeared at the door of the communications bunker, eating from a large bag of chips.

"What's all the noise . . . ?"

He trailed off when he saw the four villains. He tried to turn and run but Viral hurled a ball of smoke at him. Johnston fell as the black mist enveloped his head. He began choking, clawing at his throat as welts appeared across his face. He coughed helplessly until he finally died.

It was such a spectacle that the others had taken their eyes off Mr. Grimm. It was just enough of a distraction for him to make an attempt at freedom. Grimm disliked confrontation, and was a coward at heart, which was why he had abandoned the young Downloaders at Diablo Island. He took to the air, and immediately transformed. His face became gaunt, almost skeletal, and he zoomed through the air like a ghost—an aspect of his power that had given him his alter ego.

Basilisk launched in pursuit, ordering the others to access the Foundation's computers through the communications bunker.

Basilisk and Grimm skimmed at high speeds through the myriad glass cylinders, toward the Foundation's central buildings. Basilisk realized that Grimm wanted to take refuge in there, but it was too close for him to be able to open a portal to escape—that power only worked over long distances. Basilisk fired an energy blast that went wide—fracturing one of the canisters.

A Traitor's Revenge

Almost immediately the glutinous superpowers within seeped out; Basilisk narrowly avoided getting splattered.

Grimm weaved his way through the complex, ducking under and over high-pressure pipes in a valiant attempt to shake Basilisk. But the supervillain was too quick for him.

Basilisk took the initiative and raced ahead of Grimm's position. As he had anticipated, Grimm changed direction when he couldn't see Basilisk pursuing—then Basilisk swooped like a hawk.

Grimm was brought up short as Basilisk blocked his path. Startled, Grimm unleashed a sonic blast at him. The sound wave was visible as it erupted from Grimm's mouth and pounded into Basilisk like a fist. The villain was pitched through the air and the sound wave shattered two more of the chemical vats around Basilisk, the superpowers merging like a rainbow on the deck floor, hissing as they violently reacted with one another. Basilisk was desperate not to get any of the liquid on himself.

Mr. Grimm looked around and was relieved to find that Basilisk had vanished. He turned to flee and was surprised to see the villain hovering right behind him. Grimm didn't even have time to make a sound— Basilisk's eyes glowed brighter than ever, his powers stronger than they had been in the last fourteen years now that he had rejuvenated himself with Pete's DNA.

Grimm raised his hand—which turned to stone. He screamed, then opened a portal and slipped away from danger. He was injured and this was no longer his fight.

Viral studied the computer system in the communications bunker.

"It looks like we can access everything from here. Worm, do the honors."

"Shouldn't we wait for Basilisk?"

There was a twinkle in Viral's eye. "Nah. I'm beginning to get the impression Stone Head has a plan he's not telling us. I'll infect the system with a little backup for us, just in case he ever thinks he doesn't need us."

Eric Kirby closed his eyes when the sirens went off; it was as if he was seeing the events in his mind's eye.

"Basilisk, Trojan, Viral, and Worm. The gang is all here."

"This is it," said Toby. "The final fight." He was surprised that he wasn't frightened. During the flight to Mongolia he'd had time to think. He nodded to his friend. "Pete was right. We've been disorganized. Greedily taking whatever superpowers we thought were cool. But not this time. Now we work together. What do you think, Pete? Best way to handle this?"

A Traitor's Revenge

Pete was surprised by Toby's question. Toby had never asked his opinion about a mission before.

"Er . . . there's four of them, four of us—an even fight. We know their capabilities, so let's try to figure out how to counter some of them."

"Aren't you forgetting that Hero.com is off-line?" said Emily. "We don't have any more powers."

Eric stood and expanded his hands. "This is the *home* of Hero.com. There is no need for you to access the Internet here. This time they come straight from the source." He winked as he booted up a computer. "And they pack a *punch*!"

Basilisk joined his companions outside the communications bunker.

"Grimm has fled."

"I hate that creep," said Trojan. "I saw him at a few of the Council parties. Never trusted him."

"Viral, how long before the satellite is back online?"

"Four hours. The virus I created didn't all go through, so I can't bring it back when I want. We have to sit it out."

"Very well. Now the last phase. There was no provision for an enemy getting this far; the Foundation deemed it an impossible task. We know the Council is keeping the Enforcers busy, so this city is ours for the taking. Once we seize the control center"—he pointed to the towers in the hub—"then it's game over. Take no prisoners. Show *no* mercy."

"Giving sermons as ever, huh?"

Basilisk turned around to see Pete hovering in the air, grinning.

Basilisk snarled. "You just won't die, will you?"

"You first!" said Pete as he extended both hands, multiple laser blasts shooting from his fingers. Basilisk reacted just in time and summoned a small shield to deflect them.

Viral and Trojan both took their battle stances, but before they could do anything, Toby and Emily appeared on either side of them with a thunderclap, and unleashed their freshly gained powers.

A large bubble formed around Viral and swept him off his feet—just as he unleashed a viral agent that only polluted the air within his transparent cell, causing him to cough and gag.

Emily shot forward at superspeed and delivered some twenty punches to Trojan in a single second. The villain only had fleeting glimpses of a fist smashing her stomach, then her chin and ribs in rapid succession. She fell under the onslaught.

Worm backpedaled away, thinking he could escape. Lorna blocked his path and tutted.

"And where do you think you're going, short stuff?"

She hurled a set of glowing darts from her fingertips.

A Traitor's Revenge

But Worm reacted with surprising speed. He collapsed into a pile of earthy granules, which flowed around Lorna's feet and reformed into Worm in the blink of an eye.

Lorna's energy darts slammed into the back of Basilisk. He dropped to his knees in agony as they exploded, shredding his cloak.

Pete landed and grabbed Basilisk around the throat.

"After what you did to me, I'll definitely show no mercy!" he snarled. He had super-strength, so when Basilisk's huge stone hands gripped Pete's arms to pull him away, he resisted. Basilisk's hood slipped off and Pete gaped at what he saw. Even misshapen and scarred, he could recognize his *own* features.

"What—?"

Pete was distracted enough for Basilisk to lunge forward and head-butt him. He staggered back, and didn't see the right hook Basilisk delivered. The blow lifted Pete off his feet, and he smashed through two separate power-holding tanks. The colorful gloop cascaded out, covering him.

Toby quickly surveyed the battle and was alarmed to see Pete knocked down. Trojan had hidden beneath her cape and Emily's punches were now useless. He glanced around to see Lorna. . . .

She was being yanked off her feet by Worm. Like a wrestler, he held Lorna over his head, then body-slammed her against the deck. She skidded, winded— and then rolled off the edge of the platform!

Looking over the edge, Toby could see nothing but the clouds and mountain ranges below. He took a step toward Worm and was about to unleash a fireball when Lorna reappeared, leaping back on the platform and surprising Worm. She pointed beyond Toby.

"Tobe! Behind!"

He spun to see that Viral had beaten his way out of the energy bubble, which sagged around him like plastic sheeting.

"Nice try, kid. But you're no match for me. How about a little Ebola?" He puckered his lips and a green mist blew out, straight at Toby. But Toby had been prepared, and ensured he'd downloaded powers to tackle the flying infection.

Toby breathed in a lungful of air—then blew out with such force it was as if a whirlwind had struck Viral. The mist flew back into the villain's face, and he was plucked from his feet and smashed into a network of steel valves and pipes behind him.

Meanwhile, Basilisk flew over Pete, who was spitting out the thick, superpowered liquid.

Basilisk laughed. "That stuff will hurt, much more than *this*." He shot an energy blast at Pete, and the boy was hurled backward into another glass tank that fractured as the pressure was disrupted.

Toby ran after Viral but was floored as a plasma discus smacked into the side of his head. His vision blurred, but he could just make out Trojan crouching on a set of pipes. She hurled another plasma blast, which painfully struck his back. He hit the deck and saw that Emily was also on the floor, out for the count.

Toby gritted his teeth because of the pain. It seemed they were losing against the more experienced villains.

Worm stood over Lorna as she struggled to get her breath back. He pressed his foot against her throat, choking her. "In my day, girls knew that their place was to be unseen and silent!"

"Let her go!"

Worm's eyes grew as wide as saucers. He didn't have to look to know whose voice that was. "As I live and breathe! Commander Courage!"

Eric Kirby was standing calmly on the deck, both hands resting on his cane. "I thought I'd seen the last of you."

Worm was genuinely shocked to see how his nemesis had aged. "Commander, you look . . . so *old*. I think you did me a favor leaving me in suspended animation for all those years. I look *much* better than you."

"You couldn't look better than me, even if I were dead!"

The two adversaries circled one another. Lorna rubbed her throat, unable to say a word. But she knew the old man didn't stand a chance. Eric Kirby unsheathed a long sword blade hidden inside his cane and swished it expertly through the air. Worm retaliated by extending long thin claws from the fingertips of one hand—four blades against one.

They clashed in a whirl of claws and steel. Eric Kirby was still as nimble as an Olympic gymnast. He somersaulted over Worm's head as the villain charged—causing him to run headfirst into a set of steel pipes.

Basilisk glanced at the fight behind him, and assumed he was winning with the three kids down. He turned back, just as Pete leaped to the air like a jack-in-the-box, dripping an assortment of liquid powers that were burning his skin. His glasses had been knocked aside, but remarkably he could see perfectly.

"You're going down!" he bellowed at Basilisk.

Pete spread his arms wide and his entire body glowed

with an intense silver light—a shock wave rippled out, sending Basilisk reeling to the ground; a glass tank cushioned his fall as it shattered.

Pete burned like a supernova, forcing Worm and Eric Kirby to shield their eyes. It was enough of a distraction for Worm, who blindly lunged, cutting Kirby across his chest. The old man staggered backward.

Worm followed it with a backstroke. Kirby parried the blow and delivered a devastating swing that cleaved Worm in half.

Lorna had been watching in fascination and grimaced, expecting a lot of blood. Instead she blinked in surprise.

Worm was still alive.

The villain looked at his two halves in despair. Amazingly a brand-new lower torso formed on one half—and a duplicate upper torso on the other. It was like watching a balloon expand as the second-Worm's features slowly formed.

Then the two duplicates stared at each other and laughed.

"Two against one," they both said simultaneously. "Time for revenge!"

Eric Kirby was too astonished to defend himself as eight claws slashed at him.

"No!" screamed Lorna, and she unleashed powerful

energy darts from both hands that smashed into the duplicate villains.

At the moment Trojan was about to finish Toby off, the blinding flash from Pete caught her attention. Without a moment to lose, Toby blew his hurricane breath straight into Trojan. It caught her cape and lifted her backward against a storage tank. The glass cracked but didn't break.

Toby followed it up with a fireball that smashed across her chest and shattered the glass behind her. Trojan was lost in the wall of liquid powers, but Toby could see her arms waving as she battled to stay afloat. The liquid flooded the deck like a tidal wave.

Toby suddenly felt a new wave of energy. He was the group's leader; he couldn't let the villains win this one. They had suffered failure time and time again as Basilisk or his cronies had slipped through their fingers, kidnapped Pete, and now infiltrated the Hero Foundation headquarters.

He struggled to his feet, looking around at his battling friends. "Come on! Fight them! We can win this! We are *heroes*!"

Lorna felt surprisingly motivated by Toby's battle

cry and tore her gaze from the Worm duo to assess the situation. She noticed that Emily was lying unconscious in the path of the tidal wave.

"Em!"

The wave scooped her up and dragged her toward the edge. Lorna leaped into the air and raced forward—plucking Emily out just as she reached the rim. She watched helplessly as Trojan was swept off, limbs flailing as she fell into the clouds.

Basilisk shrieked in pain as the liquid superpowers burned his skin. He knew high dosages were dangerous, even to Primes. He had seen what moderate quantities had done to Jake Hunter, his old protégé, but Pete was practically swimming in them—absorbing the raw, undigitized powers through every pore in his skin.

Basilisk took flight but Pete swooped in and tackled him. Entwined, they both spun through the air, trading punches.

Basilisk used his petrification power on the boy, but Pete's face suddenly burned blank and featureless like a mask. It was a mass of golden energy making him resemble a living statue. He didn't feel the effect of Basilisk's powers.

"That's all you've got?" he taunted the villain.

Basilisk was amazed. "What's happened to you?"

"I've become more powerful than you can imagine!" said Pete.

They were not just empty words. Pete *felt* it.

Basilisk knew he was outclassed. But he had one trick left. He concentrated on his own body. While he could turn others to stone, Basilisk also had the power to increase his own density. He grabbed Pete around the neck and willed himself heavier.

Even with the new power he felt, Pete couldn't prevent himself from being dragged to the deck like a meteorite. He hit the steel superstructure with such force that the entire carrier rocked. The impact caused dozens of other holding tanks to smash in a wide shock wave around them. The thick fluids surged over Pete and Basilisk in a kaleidoscope of sizzling superpowers.

Toby raced toward Viral, and found the man lying at an awkward angle amid the pipes. Anywhere his body touched it, the metal was rapidly corroding, and the colorful superpower liquids squirted out at high pressure. Toby avoided the spray and prepared a fireball . . . but he hesitated. Viral looked pathetic, just like a neglected kid. He was an outcast. Toby felt a pang of sympathy. His adventures were beginning to make him wiser, and he now realized that not every situation was a black-and-white one. His sense of compassion and reasoning was truly developing.

"Don't move, we'll get you help when this is over."

Viral laughed, but the action caused pain. "Course I believe you. A nice cell on Diablo Island, right?"

"That's not what I mean."

"You were just yelling that you were a hero. You're all the same. Lock away what you don't understand."

"That's not true."

The deck shuddered again as Pete and Basilisk rolled around, locked in a deadly struggle. A loose pipe fell across Viral, causing him to howl in pain and crushing his arm.

"Understand this," he said through gritted teeth. "I have set a virus in the main computer. Something I can control remotely."

"Don't do it!"

"I never liked flying. Always preferred to have my feet on the *ground*."

Viral closed his eyes—and at that exact moment the whole Foundation carrier lumbered to one side as Viral's infection deactivated the anti-gravity system. It was like being on the deck of the *Titanic* as it sank—the carrier plummeted through the clouds, earthbound. Everybody slid down the incline.

* * *

Lorna was still holding Emily as she hovered over the Foundation complex. Smashed pipes and utility vehicles around the complex rolled down the slope and off the edge of the floating carrier.

Toby took to the air with his sister. A waterfall of debris flowed off the edge of the carrier and poured into the clouds.

Pete and Basilisk were still embraced in combat. The superpowered liquid clung to them both in thick, gloopy strands.

Then Pete suddenly extinguished his glowing appearance, reverting to normal as the carrier lurched, pouring the liquid over the edge and almost driving him and Basilisk with it.

Basilisk pushed Pete aside and took to the air, leaving the boy to slide down the slope. Pete smashed through tank after tank, more powers washing over him.

Toby darted forward like a missile to save him.

At the same moment Emily came to and noticed that Eric Kirby was sliding off the edge. He was bleeding badly but still alive. She broke from Lorna's grasp and flew toward him, grabbing his hand just as he sailed off the side.

A Traitor's Revenge

"Em, wait a minute," shouted Lorna. Then she noticed that the Worm twins were hanging from a pipe, feet flailing in the air as the incline increased. She shot forward, but before she could do anything to help, a heavy steel tower that supported pressure pipes broke away with a screech of steel and slammed into the twins. Lorna saw them burst into particles, but then a wave of congealing superpowers washed over them with an acidic hiss.

"Lorn, help me!" It was Emily. Eric Kirby's weight was dragging her back down to the sloping carrier. Lorna flew across and helped her friend.

Toby was an arm's length away from Pete as Pete smashed through another vat. A rainbow of gunk clung to Pete, and he no longer seemed conscious.

"Pete! I'm here!" screamed Toby.

He clutched his friend's sleeve, which was slick with ooze—and then felt a blast knock him sideways into a gantry. He had to shield his eyes from the sun as Basilisk dropped on him.

"You've lost!" roared Basilisk. "Don't you see I've won? The Hero Foundation is falling apart around you!"

The fact hit Toby like a physical blow. Basilisk was right. The moment they hit the ground the Foundation and Hero.com would be no more.

Basilisk pinned Toby against the pipes with his full weight. "I just wanted you to know how badly you've been defeated, before I kill you!"

Toby noticed two things at once. Pete's body was slipping over the edge in a waterfall of artificial super-powers, and that Basilisk looked vaguely like Pete, which alarmed him.

Basilisk's eyes started to glow. Toby felt his skin become instantly dry and he screamed as it cracked. Toby held up his arm to try to block Basilisk's eyes, but all that happened was that the skin on his forearm turned gray.

Toby took a deep breath—then teleported away. Basilisk stumbled and looked around, furious that he had been cheated out of the kill.

Toby reappeared slightly below the carrier, at its edge. Teleporting in the middle of the sky was an unpleasant experience as he immediately plunged, and had to initiate his flying power. He looked around for Pete and spotted him falling faster than the carrier, amid a sea of debris.

Toby spurred forward and swept up Pete, unsure if his friend was still alive. He blanked out those negative thoughts and concentrated on staying airborne with his friend's weight. Commander Courage had said the powers packed a punch. Toby just hoped he was right about that.

He was relieved to see Emily and Lorna swoop down with Eric Kirby strung between them.

"We have to get out of here!" warned Lorna.

"What?"

"The carrier . . . has a nuclear reactor . . . ," wheezed Kirby. He mimed an explosion with his fingers.

"I just used my teleport!" said Toby. He knew with Pete's additional weight there was no way he could outrun an explosion—and the carrier was seconds away from impact with the desert.

"Grab hold!" said Emily.

Toby kept a firm grip on Pete and clutched Emily's shoulder . . .

Just as the city fell from the sky.

Explosions popped across the deck as power plants overloaded. As the central hub hit the ground, the elegant towers toppled into one another like dominoes and the nuclear reactor exploded with a blinding flash.

The heroes teleported away just as an expanding radioactive shock wave tore the Hero Foundation into billions of pieces. A mushroom cloud punched a fist toward the sky as the explosion echoed across the Gobi desert.

Basilisk had been defeated for now, but the Hero command center had been destroyed.

* * *

The rhythmic bleep of a life-support machine was the only sound in the room. Toby, Lorna, and Emily stared at Pete, who was covered in bandages and motionless. They were in a sterile private room in one of the Foundation's private hospitals.

"How long will he be like this?" said Emily. Her eyes were bloodshot from crying. Toby had been surprised when she hugged him tight for comfort.

Eric Kirby stood behind them. His wounds were healed, and he wore a fresh linen suit. He still had his cane for support. He shook his head. "We don't know. He's in a very deep coma, after direct contact with so much raw hyper energy."

"I thought these powers were supposed to be safe?" snapped Lorna.

"In small doses, yes. And even in higher quantities, we Primes have a certain natural tolerance. But in a normal person . . . well, we simply don't know what effect that is going to have on him. This is unprecedented. To be honest, I'm amazed he's still alive."

Toby left the room, and stood on the small balcony that overlooked the hospital grounds. Since they had returned he had thought of nothing but the welfare of his friend. They had all contacted their parents to say they were safe and had given convincing alibis. Kirby had assured them that he would contact Pete's parents directly and inform them of their son's condition.

A Traitor's Revenge

Toby thought about how out of control things had become during the events leading to the downfall of the Hero Foundation, and he felt guilty. They had had a responsibility and they had failed.

Eric Kirby laid a hand on his shoulder.

"You did well, you know."

"We failed."

"You all saved my life. That's no failure. And you interfered with Basilisk's plans just enough to give us time to evacuate our staff to other bases."

Toby didn't understand immediately. Then he frowned. "What other bases? I thought that was the end of the Hero Foundation?"

"If I had died, it would have been. That was the Foundation's headquarters. The very first we made. And it was the *main* storage area for our powers. With those gone it's going to take a while to rebuild the collection. From that location you could control *everything*, which is why Basilisk wanted it. But we have other subbases— ones Basilisk didn't know about. They're smaller, and not as efficient, but we'll manage to get Hero.com back online soon, even if it runs at a limited capacity until we can rebuild a new HQ."

"The other bases, where are they?" said Toby, relieved to find a glimmer of hope.

"We created them around the four elements. That's *air* destroyed. But the location of the others is a secret for now, I'm sorry. Once we get the satellite back we can reach other Downloaders so they can finally begin to fight back. And their bravery will bring the Primes out of hiding and ready to fight. If it hadn't been for you four stalling Basilisk, we would have lost *everything*."

Toby grinned, relieved that they *had* made a difference. Mr. Grimm stepped onto the balcony and whispered something in Kirby's ear. Then they both excused themselves.

Everybody was surprised that Grimm had survived, although Toby guessed that he'd probably teleported away at the first sign of danger.

Kirby paused before he left the room.

"You should all go home and rest. We'll let you know the moment Pete's condition changes."

Toby only wished his friend was better, then life would be back to normal. Well, normal for them. He was convinced Pete would pull through, and when he did, Toby promised himself that he wouldn't be such a control freak over using Hero.com. His friendship was more important. And they could be a team once more—doing what they did best.

The door opened again. Toby was expecting another nurse to enter, but was surprised when he heard Lorna shriek with delight. Her boyfriend had arrived.

Toby took a deep breath and walked into the room.

A Traitor's Revenge

He stopped in utter shock when he saw the new arrival. The last person he had expected to see.

Jake Hunter.

Toby didn't yet know that Lorna had just led them all into a world of trouble—one that would alter their lives forever. . . .

Andy Briggs was born in Liverpool, England. Having endured many careers, ranging from pizza delivery and running his own multimedia company to teaching IT and filmmaking (though not all at the same time), he eventually remembered the constant encouragement he had received at an early age about his writing. That led him to launch himself on a poor, unsuspecting Hollywood. In between having fun writing movie scripts, Andy now has far too much fun writing novels.

He lives in a secret lair somewhere in the southeast of England——attempting to work despite his two crazy cats. His claims about possessing superpowers may be somewhat exaggerated. . . .

Tired of being a goody-goody all the time?

Ready to get in touch with your dark side?

Luckily, Andy Briggs, the courageous mastermind behind
VIRUS ATTACK, has a dark side too. Join him in the continued
struggle for world domination in:

Dark
Hunter

Turn the page for a teaser chapter, and prepare to find your
inner supervillain!

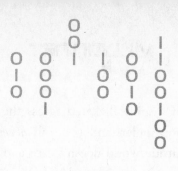

The Great Escape

WHAM! Jake's head jerked back with the powerful blow to his cheek. He had a metallic taste in his mouth: his lip must be bleeding. Through a swollen eye he looked at Chameleon sitting across the table.

The superhero had been interrogating Jake since he'd arrived at Diablo Island Penitentiary, three . . . four weeks ago? Maybe more—days had blurred into one another.

Chameleon motioned for the heavy Enforcer to stop hitting the boy. The man was huge, dressed in the uniform worn by the United Nations' secret army whose mission was to conceal superheroes from public awareness and to capture supervillains. Like Jake.

"Had enough, Hunter?" said Chameleon.

Jake glared at the young man across the table, who was dressed in immaculate black and sporting a sharp haircut with a widow's peak. Chameleon could shapeshift, but this seemed to be his normal form.

"When I get out of here," Jake said through cracked lips, "I'll kill you."

A ghost of a smile flickered across the hero's face. "Fine. But you understand you will *never* get out of here. The outside world doesn't care and your family have forgotten you *ever* existed."

Jake tried to lunge forward, but he was bound to the chair and feeling weak because he hadn't been able to download powers from Villain.net. Those superpowers kept him alive. Whatever powerless replacement Chameleon was pumping into him was doing nothing more than keeping him tired and weak.

"I saved your family," continued the hero. "They will no longer have the heartbreak of suffering such an insolent son as you."

Jake jerked futilely in the chair and the Enforcer raised a threatening hand to strike again, but pulled away when Chameleon gave a slight shake of the head. The hero had never physically struck Jake during the interrogations, but he was more than happy to allow the Enforcers to be heavy-handed.

"I'll get them back," spat Jake. "Then I'll kill you and all your little superfriends when I tear this place apart!"

Chameleon smiled, and Jake wanted to rip his smug face off.

"Your family is gone, Hunter. And restoring their memories is not a power that even you possess." He paused. "I think by now I'm starting to believe you don't know the location of the Council of Evil."

The Great Escape

The Council of Evil was a dedicated group of supervillains who had created an empire in retaliation to the Hero Foundation. Classic evil versus good. Both sides had started recruiting heroes and villains through Hero.com and Villain.net, and both sides had successfully hidden their headquarters away from the other.

"I've never been," growled Jake. "And if I had, I'd slaughter them too! Basilisk did this to me, made me dependent on that stupid Web site!"

"He did more than that, Hunter, and you know it. Your body has become entangled with Villain.net. And that's what makes you valuable to both sides."

"I told you before: I don't care!"

"You have the unique ability to absorb powers from Villain.net, far greater than experts previously thought was possible. But not only that, you can create new ones that we've never seen before."

Jake laughed. This was the usual sermon from Chameleon, but it didn't change the fact that Jake had been tied to a chair every day and beaten for information.

Chameleon leaned forward, tenderness flashing across his face. "Hunter . . . Jake, please. Work with us, not against us. Use your abilities to help the Hero Foundation. Together we can eradicate evil and make the world a much better place."

Jake took a moment to contemplate Chameleon's

offer, but it was a simple decision—there was only one important person. Himself.

With the limited movement available to him, Jake twisted his hand and threw an obscene gesture and a charming smile.

The look of fury on the hero's face was worth the punch across the face from the Enforcer.

The silence was so deep that Jake could hear the blood pounding in his ears. He'd been mentally counting the minutes since they had thrown him back into his cell. The lighting was so intentionally bright that it was impossible to tell where the floor met the walls, and it hurt Jake's eyes and made his photosensitive skin tingle unpleasantly. Aside from his addiction to Villain.net, that was another side effect of his DNA being entangled with the super-power system.

Jake was now feeling stronger than he had been when Chameleon had first apprehended him on the beach of Basilisk's volcanic island. Perhaps there was something in the replacement power they'd been using to keep him alive. But now Jake had had enough. His craving for superpowers was too strong. It didn't matter what the powers were—they always made him feel stronger and more alive. And his body was a cauldron of hyperenergy, sloshing it all around to give him useful if unexpected powers. Most of the time.

He had decided it was time to leave.

On his first night on Diablo Island he had found a cell phone tucked under the pillow in his chamber. On it was a link to access the Villain.net Web site, and he knew from past experience that he could download limited powers from this device. But he had resisted using the phone in case it was some kind of trap set up by Chameleon.

The second night he had received a text message on the phone telling him not to delay escaping. The message was just signed "Your Caring Benefactor."

He had no idea who that person was. He'd speculated it could be Basilisk, who had claimed they were now genetic twins, *almost* clones. But why would the archfiend help? Jake had sworn revenge after he'd made him addicted to Villain.net.

Now, as midnight approached and the Enforcers who patrolled the cellblock had returned to their barracks for a scheduled break, Jake pulled the cell phone from under his pillow and stared at the screen. His fingers trembled, both from excitement at the prospect of escaping, and from a lack of strength. He pushed the control pad to highlight the Villain.net link, a lengthy mixture of foreign alphabets and numbers, and clicked on it.

Within seconds the screen changed to a miniature version of the Web site. There was a list of icons, all representing superpowers and all too small to identify . . .

He blindly chose several powers and saw a thin tendril warp out of the screen and tap him on the forehead. Then a sensation like pins and needles rippled through his body and he went from being weak and lethargic to feeling as if he could conquer the world.

Jake leaped off his bed and stretched his arms, feeling the blood flow to his muscles and his mind sharpen to primeval alertness. He had gleaned a little information from the Enforcer guards who escorted him to and from his cell each day. They had talked freely, assuming that Jake was no longer a threat. His cell walls were a few feet thick, and at the end of the corridor, which was lined with security cameras, lay an open courtyard where some prisoners were permitted to exercise, although Jake had never been allowed outside. He was being housed in the minimal security wing; after all, he was now just a boy with no superpowers. Hardly a threat to Diablo Island Penitentiary—the very name of which made seasoned supervillains tremble.

Jake tucked the phone into his jeans pocket—the same worn black jeans he'd been wearing for weeks. He knew that the moment the alarms were triggered, hundreds of heavily armed Enforcers would be upon him, and he wasn't sure he had the strength to fight them all. The situation called for a tactical approach.

His fingers traced the edges of the cell door in the hope he could find a gap, but it was made with such precision it could have been airtight. Jake was beginning to think he'd have to resort to brute force when the lock suddenly clicked open as he moved his hand across it. Puzzled, Jake gently pulled the door open and stepped out into the dark corridor beyond. He experimentally waved his hand across the lock several times and each time it slid back and forth through some kind of telekinesis.

"Now that's cool," Jake murmured to himself, shutting the door behind him.

He looked around the corridor and immediately identified three surveillance cameras. He wafted his hand like he was swatting a fly, and all three cameras quickly snapped aside, as if he'd physically struck them.

Jake stealthily approached the double security doors ahead, his mind running through his options. His overwhelming urge was to find Chameleon, who he knew was somewhere on the island, and exact his revenge. But the new cautious side of Jake's mind urged him to flee as quickly as possible. He might have superpowers, but nobody had yet managed to escape from Diablo Island, as he was constantly reminded.

As he took several more steps to freedom the double

doors suddenly gave a loud beep and began to slide apart—somebody was coming in! Evidently he had miscounted while lying in his cell, and this was the scheduled security patrol. Fighting panic, he moved into the shadows—and felt a sensation just like falling into water. He gave a startled yelp as he saw his body transform and disappear into the pool of blackness. His head popped from the shadows on the floor, just enough to comprehend he had become part of them. Two Enforcers had entered, weapons cradled in their arms. They walked past Jake without noticing him, both doing bad impressions of a TV comedian they had just been watching.

Jake gave silent thanks that, by chance, he had the right powers to slide him out unnoticed. Then a second thought hit him—perhaps his mysterious benefactor had ensured that he'd downloaded exactly the powers he'd need, just like Basilisk had done before.

Basilisk. Again that name brought a wave of anger. Jake was sure that he wanted to kill the villain on sight, and he figured Basilisk realized this. The fiend was responsible for ruining his life, getting him imprisoned— everything that was bad in Jake's life had been a direct consequence of Basilisk's involvement. But if it wasn't Basilisk helping him out, then who could it possibly be?

His benefactor's identity would have to wait until he got clear of Diablo Island. In fact, he had no idea where the island was located geographically. He clambered out of the shadows, as easily as pulling himself out of a swimming pool, and ran through the doors just as they were closing.

He was outside for the first time in days, standing in a courtyard half the size of a football field. The first thing that struck him was the intense cold and heavy falling snow. It felt like being back in Moscow again. The second thing he noticed was that it was night, but the courtyard was bathed in brilliant floodlights. An alarm suddenly sounded.

An Enforcer in a watchtower had opened the door for his two colleagues to enter the minimum-security wing, and he had watched them step inside without incident. When he looked at his bank of monitors to confirm they were safely inside, he was surprised to see that the images coming from the corridor showed blank walls. He tore his gaze from the screen and back into the courtyard in time to see Jake run out. The doors closed behind the boy, and the Enforcer punched a bright-red alarm button.

"Aw, geez," Jake groaned as the sound of whooping sirens erupted across the complex. This was exactly what he wanted to avoid. He shielded his eyes from the floodlights and saw an Enforcer aim his gun.

"On the ground now or I'll open fire!" yelled the guard.

Jake reacted on impulse and extended his hands, hoping something spectacular would happen. He wasn't disappointed.

An enormous energy sphere formed between both hands and he lobbed it like a bowling ball. The energy sphere smashed into the legs of the watchtower, tearing two of the steel supports away. The entire structure toppled over with a wail of stressed steel. The tower struck a wall halfway up its length, and the momentum pitched the Enforcer hard to the floor.

More guards ran from doors opposite Jake, and he heard the doors to the minimum-security wing begin to rumble open behind him. He spun around and formed another energy sphere—slamming it into the door with such force that the steel buckled, preventing it from opening any farther.

By the time he turned back around to see the growing army of angry Enforcers, a hail of bullets had impacted inches from him—all stopped by a translucent energy shield that expanded from his body and rippled with each hit. Jake was not sure how long the shield would last—the number of bullets increased with such ferocity that he was soon facing a wall of lead. It obscured his view like insects on a car windshield. The clatter of falling shells was almost as loud as the gunshots.

Jake walked forward, but the weight of the bullets made it feel like he was walking through molasses. He

The Great Escape

blindly lobbed another energy sphere. It must have struck some Enforcers as the gunfire abated and he heard screams.

A voice echoed around from the prison's PA system. "Jake Hunter, you have been identified and will be terminated if you do not surrender!"

Yeah, great options, thought Jake.

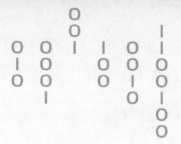